Beth cannot believe what she is hearing.

"Beth, Beth, I have to know. . .is Harold my son?" William blurted out desperately and jumped to his feet.

She stared up at him blankly. He could see she was trying to comprehend his question. He knew when the implication of what he was asking suddenly hit her. Her eyes widened and every drop of color drained from her face.

She sprang to her feet. Her mouth opened and then closed as though she could not speak. Absolute horror filled her eyes.

"You. . .you. . .how dare you. . .dare you ask. . .such a dreadful thing!" she whispered at last.

William knew he had his answer. He also knew he had just made the most dreadful mistake any husband could make.

"You gave him the name John for his second name," he added in a daze, at long last bringing into the open what had perhaps convinced him the most, hurt him the most.

"John?" Her voice sounded as though it came from a great distance. "It was my own father's. . .my father's. . ."

"Beth. . ."

His choked, horrified whisper barely registered with Beth.

Trembling violently, she started shaking her head from side to side in violent negation that he could even think such a horrible thing of her. Fear was replaced by a sudden dreadful anger all mixed up with unbearable pain of heart and body.

Through a thick haze she saw William's hand go out to her. She raised her hand and struck out at it. She missed, but she whirled around and strode off, not caring where she went, just knowing she had to get away from him.

MARY HAWKINS has thoroughly enjoyed the ups and downs of thirty-four years of being a minister's wife at churches in various cities in New South Wales and Queensland, Australia. She and husband Ray have two married sons and one daughter, and are still waiting to be grandparents.

Mary has long had a dream to write an historical series. "The Great Southland" series is the combination of her dream with details from family history. For Mary, the wonder of readers enjoying her writing efforts is a constant source of praise to the Lord Jesus she loves.

Books by Mary Hawkins

HEARTSONG PRESENTS
HP42—Search for Tomorrow
HP101—Damaged Dreams
HP129—Search for Yesterday
HP202—Search for Today
HP316—Faith in the Great Southland
HP320—Hope in the Great Southland

Don't miss out on any of our super romances. Write to us at the following address for information on our newest releases and club information.

Heartsong Presents Readers' Service
PO Box 719
Uhrichsville, OH 44683

Love
in the Great Southland

Mary Hawkins

Heartsong Presents

Many thanks goes to my family researchers and the information in their books *Pedlers of Australia 1838–1986* and *From the Borders to the Bush: A Telfer Family History.*

My darling husband, Ray Hawkins, wrote Beth's poem, "I Love You" and "Three Loves." I have also used sections from one of his marriage services. And of course, he has kindly given me his personal permission to use them all!

To my dear mother, Gladys Pedler, and the Pedler and Telfer pioneers of South Australia.

A note from the author:
I love to hear from my readers! You may correspond with me by writing:
    Mary Hawkins
    Author Relations
    PO Box 719
    Uhrichsville, OH 44683

ISBN 1-57748-549-1

LOVE IN THE GREAT SOUTHLAND

Cover illustration by Dominick Saponaro.

PRINTED IN THE U.S.A.

prologue

England, April 1835

The public gallery in the courtroom was hot, stifling. The crowd squeezed in around her were restless, excited, yelling out curses on the white-faced prisoner now standing in the dock. She stared at the tall, handsome figure, not taking her eyes for a moment from this man she had befriended just a few months ago, a lonely man, a strong man, but a gentle one.

The judge's gavel thundered again and again. The crowd around her subsided. Their stillness frightened her even more. She looked apprehensively around, but no one was paying her heavily veiled person any attention. Every eye was avidly fixed on Judge Wedgewood.

"John Martin, you have just been found guilty of the felonious slaying of Lord Farnley's gamekeeper, Jock Macallister."

An excited buzz swept through the crowd. Her tears that had been so very close spilled over. A desperate sob whelmed up and tore past her throat.

It was not true. It could not be true. He had often said how much he admired old Jock, had spoken so affectionately about him during their stolen moments together. Surely he would not, could not, have killed old Jock?

Suddenly she realized several heads had swung toward her, trying to peer through her veil, wondering who this strange woman was who seemed to have some sympathy for the felon. Her hand held the heavy veil to her lips, stifling the next sob that was threatening.

"Do you have anything to say before I pronounce your sentence?"

At the judge's ponderous words, her eyes swung back to the man in the dock. She froze, hardly daring to breathe. His eyes seemed to be looking straight at her. But no, they moved on as though desperately searching for just one friendly face. His shoulders suddenly went back. He stood stiffly, even as he had that last day when she. . .they. . .

"As God is my witness, I declare once more that I am not guilty!"

She believed him. Who could not believe that ringing, slightly accented voice that had spoken such tender, comforting words to her when she had needed them so much. Her mind blocked out the exchange between him and the judge, fleeing from the pain in him, from the oppressive heat of the crowded place, the smell of sweating, excited humanity. And suddenly she was back in the green meadow at Fleetwood, in his arms, letting firm lips touch hers until. . .

Another hushed murmur brought her attention sharply back to the scene she had been staring at with unseeing eyes.

The judge had something in his hands. A black cap. She stared at it with increasing horror and jumped when the judge called out in his loud voice that reached to every inch of this courtroom.

"Prisoner at the bar! Have you anything to urge why sentence of death should not be passed upon you?"

What was he saying? What was he saying?

Her eyes clung to John Martin. Surely now he would tell them. . .tell them. . .

He was staring pleadingly, desperately down at someone in a row at the front of the courtroom. Then a slight frown, almost a puzzled look, briefly crossed that handsome face before he once more looked steadily across at the judge.

She leaned forward, trying to see who he had been staring at. Percival Farnley. Astonishment touched her. What was

Percy doing here?

She drew back quickly. He must not see her. He would tell William for sure—perhaps even Father, and he was already so upset about Mother.

"I have said all I can, Your Honor, except to declare once again my complete innocence, and pray that one day the guilty man will be found."

The prisoner's voice was so calm, so steady. Relief swept through her. Yes. . .surely now they must believe him.

But the judge. . .what was he saying?

"It is in my power to sentence you to hang by the neck until you are dead for such a heinous crime."

"Oh, no, no, not that!" She was on her feet, her voice so long silenced ringing out. Pleading. Nausea swept over her. Vaguely she knew John was again looking in her direction, searching for her. And she had failed him.

Percival Farnley was looking right at her, an evil, gloating smile twisting his lips. But she no longer cared. She felt so ill. Nausea had been creeping over her in waves. She had to get out of here now. . .away. . .

The judge was still speaking, pronouncing sentence, his words drifting to her as she frantically pushed her way through the crowd. "Mercy on you. . .transported. . .the great Southland of Australia. . .term of your natural life."

He would not hang. He would live.

Thankfulness swept through her. Then the nausea welled up, fiercer than ever. John would exist for a lifetime in hopelessness. . .in a living hell. . .

It was her last thought as she started to retch, and then was violently, shamefully sick.

one

South Australia
late February 1838

It was a strange time and place to make the discovery that she loved her husband. Loved him. . .and not just as any dutiful Christian wife should—even in an arranged marriage.

She loved William. Loved him deeply. Loved him passionately. Loved him so much she would die if he never learned to love her a fraction as much.

Beth drew in a sudden gasp of air as though her lungs had been too long deprived.

"Are you all right, Mrs. Garrett?"

She turned and looked blankly at the curious face of the woman sitting beside her on the uncomfortable plank of wood that served as a pew. Beth blinked, nodded, and forced a smile she hoped was reassuring before turning back to stare once more at William.

At someone else's wedding she discovers she loves her husband?

Tears blurred the scene in front of her. There should be moonlight, music playing, roses. There were none of those. The morning sun was already very hot, not even a violin had been found for this wedding, and there were certainly no roses, only masses of eucalyptus gum leaves, with their own peculiar fragrance, heaped in makeshift containers.

"Today is a beautiful highlight in your lives."

Beth started. *Oh, yes! It is, it is. But only if. . .*

The Reverend William Garrett was staring earnestly down at the young couple he had just pronounced husband and wife.

With a swift movement he raised that strong, handsome head and looked around the small gathering of wedding guests crammed into the roughly built bark and mud house surrounded by dense bush. His glance lingered on the sweet face of his young wife.

Beth stared at him, devouring him with her eyes. She was oblivious to the primitive surroundings. William's glance lingered on her own face for far too short a moment. Their eyes caught and clung. Something flashed in his dark depths before he looked quickly away, back to the bride and groom in front of him.

She had known him, been such good friends with him since she was a child and he a tall, gangly youth. Ever since that first day they had met. . .

What a fool I've been! she thought passionately and then realized she was trembling quite violently.

She looked swiftly around, wondering if she had spoken the words out loud. Mrs. Young was still watching her with a slight frown. Beth nodded at her and then looked quickly away, taking another deep, careful breath.

Certainly she had always loved William in some way, but never with this heart-wrenching, soul-twisting love, this intense longing to be the recipient of his sole attention. She had intensely admired him ever since she had been that apprehensive, shy little girl meeting him that very first day her new stepfather, Lord Farnley, had taken her and her mother home with him to live at Fleetwood. After he had been introduced as Lord Farnley's ward, the son of his deceased cousin, William had suddenly smiled at her so sweetly, so reassuringly, that she had suddenly known she could be happy after all in this new, unexpected life.

Of course, her new stepsister had also been there, but at first poor Kate, closer to her own age than William, had been naturally resentful of a new mother and sister being thrust upon her without any prior warning by her thoughtless father and only a bare twelve months after the death of her own beloved mother.

During those first traumatic weeks of settling into a new opulent lifestyle on the prosperous estate, it had been William who had taken Beth under his wing, so much so it had set the pattern for the years that followed.

When he had been away studying for the ministry, she had missed him every day. Even then he had still been her champion, still the one person above all others she could call on in time of need.

Except that once.

That time when he had been desperately studying and taking his final examinations. That time her mother had become seriously ill and Beth had been barred from the sickroom and left to her own devices. That time she had, out of sheer loneliness and unhappiness, made another friend, a very unwise one.

Beth shuddered.

How selfish and spoiled she had been, bemoaning her solitary days when everyone's attention was being given to the mistress of Fleetwood. She had been very young, but at least her selfishness had not caused her to intrude on William's life and study. It was small comfort.

Certainly at that time it had been carefully kept from her how ill her mother really was, but she had been lonely, feeling sadly misused and isolated when she had wanted so desperately to help nurse her mother, to be needed.

And that was when she had first met the gamekeeper's handsome young assistant. John Martin, the intense young man with that slight, Spanish accent and his intriguing stories of another land had fascinated her. He had been lonely too, and because she knew her stepfather would not have countenanced her friendship with one of his farm laborers, it had been rather exciting meeting him secretly.

A wry smile tilted her lips. She had been just sixteen and thought she was falling in love with John Martin.

Love?

That had not been love. This was love. This heart-wrenching feeling of tenderness, this need to always be near William, to touch him, and when he was away, that feeling that she was incomplete—that was love. To have him need her, to have those puzzling, undefinable barriers between them dissolve. . .

"Within the ceremony of marriage, you have made your commitment to each other in the sight of God and before witnesses. You are about to make a new life together. This life will be something entirely new to each of you."

William's rich tones washed over her. A deep longing to start anew with him filled her, to live over again the last couple years and more.

She automatically moved her position a little to ease a sudden twinge in her back, only to suddenly still again. The volume of his voice was increasing in a passionate way she had never heard before in one of his wedding sermons.

"You will face new dimensions of love and joy. There will continue to be new challenges and new opportunities to appreciate God's grace in your lives."

Why, William was now looking at her again, but so. . .so strangely. For one long moment, Beth's eyes clung to his before he swiftly looked away and down at the young couple starting out on their own great adventure.

New dimensions of love. The words hammered their way deep into Beth's heart and soul. They expressed so clearly the confused feelings that were sweeping through her. New dimensions. . . But then that meant love had been there all along, that now its boundaries were merely changing, expanding.

A delicious shiver swept through her. Of course she had always loved him, but certainly not like this, not with this consuming passion.

She saw William swallow and clear his throat as though searching for some control. She studied his face intently. It was a face so familiar and yet suddenly not at all really known to her. He was certainly tanned by the months on board ship and the harsh, hot sun of this new Southland. His cheeks were leaner, his strong jaw seemed more pronounced, as did the lines on his face.

She had noticed only this morning that there seemed to be an added tenseness in him but had put it down to today's special responsibilities, perhaps even the nearness of being a father once again and worry for her in these new, primitive surroundings.

The muscle in her back was aching again from sitting so long, and one hand went to the swell of her body where their second child lay nestled. Only a couple weeks more and their litle family would no longer be just the two of them and little Harold.

Her husband. Her son. Her family. Thankfulness and praise welled up in her.

Suddenly William's face softened, changing so swiftly from that solemn, earnest expression as he smiled so gently, so lovingly down at the couple before him. Once again Beth forgot any momentary physical discomfort as a surge of emotion horribly like envy swept through her.

How long has it been since he smiled at me, really smiled at me with that devastating dimple in his cheek, those gleaming brown eyes twinkling so brightly? she thought sadly.

If only he would smile at her anywhere near as lovingly as he just had to the blushing young bride and her proud yet bashful young groom. Not even on their own wedding day had he smiled at her like that.

She shuddered and closed her eyes.

But then their wedding had been arranged, orchestrated by Lord Farnley, even to the actual ceremony being held beside her mother's bed. It had been such a rushed affair, only a few days after William had returned home as a fully ordained minister at last, with the news of an appointment to a church in London.

And the day he had arrived home had been the very day her

father had told her at last just how ill her mother was. The doctors had given up hope weeks before, and now it was a matter of days, hours. Without waiting for her to recover from the shock of the confirmation of what she had already suspected, Lord Farnley had coldly informed her of her mother's dearest wish—to see her daughter happily married.

"I know you are still young, but it is the very last thing you can do for her," Lord Farnley had informed Beth in that icy, controlled voice that she had hated and dreaded so much, knowing he was trying only to be strong for the wife he loved.

And as she had so many times in the past, she had turned to William, and he had not failed her. He had been so pale, so stiff and formal, kindly pretending, informing her that he had her stepfather's permission to pay his addresses to her. Not then, or since, had either of them ever mentioned that their marriage had been arranged by Lord Farnley.

Beth frowned. It had not been until several days after their wedding that she had realized the Reverend William Garrett was a different man from her old lighthearted playmate and mentor. Indeed, William had changed so much that she had been forced to the conclusion that being an ordained man of the cloth had made him more aware of his responsibilities to society and the church he served and thus made him more austere, more dignified.

She had thought that they would become so much closer as a married couple. Instead it seemed as though being married had raised some insurmountable barrier between them. Of course, so quickly after their wedding, she had been devastated by her mother's death, and soon after that, she had been sick and tired with a difficult pregnancy.

She had often thought it had been no wonder the old, fun-loving William she had known had retreated more and more from a sick watering pot of a wife who had so quickly lost her shape as well as her temper.

After Harold had arrived, she had so hoped having a child

would bring them closer together. Instead it had seemed to only increase the distance, that strange barrier between them. Certainly William was a good father in so many ways, but he still withheld himself from enjoying his son, even from spending too much time with him.

But then, these last few months on board ship crossing the 15,000 miles of ocean between England and South Australia, she had seen the way he had opened up with Kate and their new friend, Adam Stevens. But as much as he had seemed to be his old self with them, he had been even more reserved with herself, even more so with Harold, until she had gone from bewilderment to anger, and now to deep pain and a resolve to find out why.

But since they had been virtually stranded here in this new colony more than a month ago, instead of being able to sail on to New South Wales as they had planned, there had been so little real time alone together. They had been so desperately busy trying to organize their permanent accommodations before the baby arrived.

"We've done it," she thought with satisfaction, "moved into our own home at last, no longer roughing it in that tent in the Youngs' clearing so close to their crowded one."

After their momentous decision to settle here for at least a couple years, they had bought their ten acres permitted by the emigration commissioner. They had been blessed in that it had already been owned by one family who had started clearing the land and had half built the primitive stone dwelling before the husband and sole provider of that family had died. The grieving wife had quickly sold it to raise the fare to return to familiar England and relatives.

William had been working so hard to finish the sturdy house. It was still primitive and lacked many of the comforts they had taken for granted in England, but for the first time in many months they were in their own home.

Perhaps now she would be able to persuade William to talk,

to really talk to her about what was troubling him. She knew it was going to take a good deal of courage to confront him. In truth, after Kate and Adam had left on their journey overland to New South Wales, she had been plain scared to start talking to William about their relationship in case it only made everything worse. Night and day she had been praying for strength, for the right words.

She had insisted on accompanying him today, despite the frowns she knew could be directed at her by those who disapproved of her going out-of-doors in her advanced condition. When Mrs. Young had told her their oldest daughter, Bessie, would be more than happy to mind Harold with her own children, she had grasped the opportunity.

It had only been a relatively short drive in the old cart, at the moment their only mode of transport. The track here had been almost nonexistent, weaving in and around trees, and the jolting over the rough ground had been much worse than she had anticipated. But the chance to share in this, his very first service in their new home, had been too enticing. She was determined to prove to him she could be a good minister's wife even in this primitive place on the outskirts of Adelaide if he decided to minister here.

And then as the wedding ceremony had commenced, she had realized how long it had been since she had been able to simply indulge herself in watching him, listening to him. It had been so many months since he had preached. On board ship the captain had not been at all sympathetic to church services, so they had met informally for prayer and reading Scripture.

She had been so filled with happiness watching and listening as the vows had been made by the young couple. William's beautiful voice had sent delicious shivers through her. She was so proud of him. It had been absolute bliss until. . .until she had realized. . .now knew. . .

Tears burned at the back of her eyes as desolation filled her. There had been times in the beginning when William had told her lightly that of course he loved her. But he had not been so gallant for months now. In fact, ever since Harold had been born he had been different. And suddenly, she passionately, quite desperately longed for him to not just mouth the words of love, but mean them!

"I would like you to reflect on the meaning of marriage," William's deep tones rumbled, drawing her wayward thoughts back to the wedding ceremony. With some shame she realized she had missed some of his message and forced herself to pay attention so she could comment knowledgeably about it afterward as a good minister's wife should.

"It may be easy to enjoy the event, but sometimes it is more difficult to appreciate the reality behind the event." Once again the Reverend Garrett raised his head, slowly this time, and looked directly at his wife. "Marriage is a commitment to love," he added softly, "but what is love?"

Beth stiffened. William had always been very, very serious about commitment. What was he saying? And why was he looking at her so intently?

"In the first book of Corinthians in the Holy Scriptures, chapter thirteen is known as the love chapter. Wherever the old word charity appears, I am going to take the liberty of substituting the word love, which is its true meaning." The slightest of smiles lightened his face once again before he looked away from her and down at the small, well-used Bible in his hand.

He started to read the familiar words she had heard him quote numerous times before at weddings. Never before had he used the word *love*. At first she thought that was what made him seem different from all the other times he had read this passage. But suddenly she realized it was far more than that. For a fleeting moment she thought she might be mistaken, that it must be because of her newly discovered love that she thought he was different. But then she knew it was not just her.

William was different. There was an added emphasis on each word, his voice rising louder with a growing passion as he quoted "Love suffereth long, and is kind; love envieth not. . ."

He paused and once again looked directly across at her. She hardly heard the next few verses that he quoted from memory, his eyes never leaving hers. It seemed as though there were only the two of them present. A tremor swept through her.

William paused for a long moment, but his gaze never wavered from his wife. No one moved. In the utter stillness, the final verse was spoken softly, with a depth of reverence that had even more impact than his triumphant, ringing tones.

"And now abideth faith, hope, love, these three." He stopped again, swallowed, and then almost whispered, "But the greatest of these is love."

Still no one stirred.

A moment longer William stared at Beth. How his heart was aching. He could see her wide, startled eyes, the blush that was rising in her beautiful face.

The young bridegroom gave a nervous little cough. William pulled himself together and glanced swiftly around. A wave of restlessness had started to rustle through the wedding guests. Wondering looks were being exchanged. A couple folk were glancing from him to Beth, and he took a deep breath and rather abruptly concluded the service with a brief prayer.

When the newly married couple were at last receiving the felicitations of their family and friends, William started toward Beth. He had only taken a step when the bride's father stepped in front of him and held out his hand.

"Reverend, a great service, a great service. We are so pleased you agreed to do this for us here at home and for going to all the trouble you did to clear it with the authorities, like." The man beamed, and William felt the coins being thrust into his hand. Before he could protest, the man had turned his back and was moving back to the bridal party.

William hesitated. He had absolutely no need of this assisted emigrant's hard-earned money, but he knew that the man's pride would be hurt if he refused it. As well, it would make people wonder about this strange minister who refused remuneration for his services! He had no desire to be seen to flaunt his and Beth's prosperity.

He shrugged and slipped the money into his pocket, knowing there would be other opportunities to help this poor family. Slowly, almost reluctantly, he turned away and started again toward where Beth had been seated. But she had gone.

It had been very hot in the crowded building. Sudden anxiety for her in her delicate condition made him quicken his pace, pushing his way as fast and politely as he could past those who would liked to have engaged him in conversation.

Beth was sitting by herself in the shade on the stump of an old gum tree and was vigorously fanning herself. He paused for a moment, studying this woman he had been married to now for so long, and yet whom it seemed he had always loved. Heavy with child, his child, she was more beautiful than ever to him.

But she was so young, so small and frail-looking. The gown she was wearing had long, fitted sleeves that seemed to emphasize the slenderness of her arms. She had still not completely recovered from the stresses of the long sea voyage, and he was worried about her. This morning she had been so pale, seeming more fragile then ever. He had not wanted her to come, but she had been so adamant that he had found himself weakly yielding when she had turned those incredibly beautiful blue eyes on him and stated indignantly, "Miss your very first service here in the Great Southland? Never, sir!"

He had smiled slightly. Ever since their wedding, she had made up her mind to be "the best minister's wife ever" as she had earnestly told him. He did not feel like smiling now. Per-haps one day she might realize he just wanted her to be herself, not fill some role others put her in.

As always, she had paid careful attention to her toilet. Despite his urgings that the layers of petticoats in the full skirt were not suitable for this hot weather, she had insisted on dressing in one of the fashionable gowns she had brought from London.

She heard his steps on the rough gravel track and looked up at him. A strange, unfamiliar look flashed across her pale face. Then, as he halted a little distance from her, she frowned and moved uncomfortably.

Suddenly he wished she was again the twelve-year-old who had hero-worshiped him, who would have bounced up and hugged him, hung on his arm, who would have told him how wonderful the service had been, how wonderful he had been.

Instead, her frown increased and she asked sharply, "What was that all about, William?"

two

William's hands clenched. Had he been so obvious? All he had been able to think of all through the wretched service had been how much he had wanted Beth to look at him at their own wedding with even a small amount of the worshipful adoration that this young bride had for her bridegroom. Instead, Beth had been extremely pale as she had stood beside him in that sad sickroom, repeating her vows in a trembling whisper. He had never been able to forget that dreadful, blind look in her eyes.

He moved closer and held out both hands to her. "What do you mean?" he heard himself murmur, and even to his own ears his voice sounded stilted. In a louder voice he said, "Come, we must get you out of this heat."

She did not stir. Her beautiful blue eyes surveyed him intently. "You. . .you were staring at me so strangely during the service."

"Was I?" he forced himself to say lightly.

"Yes," she said shortly. "People were looking at us. Some still are. It is most embarrassing."

"Then I suggest you let me help you to your feet so we may smile at these 'people' and then be on our way."

Beth studied him carefully. To her dismay, he was avoiding her eyes, standing there with his hands still held out. Reluctantly she reached up and let him take a firm grip so he could haul her ungainly body upright.

"I can manage," she said through gritted teeth. But then, as she let him help her to her feet, she felt that muscle in her back clench once again and for a moment was glad of his support. He steadied her and then released her quickly and turned away.

She caught her breath and stared at his broad back. He was

never so careless of her. It was almost as though he could not bear to touch her. The familiar stab of pain shot through her, but with it was mingled anger and frustration.

Her chin went up. With a rustle of her skirts she moved as swiftly after him as her body would allow. No way was she going to let him cause her to be the recipient of more curious looks.

She latched onto his arm and gave it a fierce little tug. He turned toward her, and she fiercely hated the politely raised eyebrow.

Raising her chin a little higher, she said angrily, "William, I will not, cannot stand this attitude of yours one more moment, and I demand—"

"Oh, Reverend Garrett, such a beautiful service. I swear your words brought me to tears."

Beth stopped abruptly. William looked relieved at the interruption. Gritting her teeth, she watched the polite smile move his lips as he turned around and graciously, if humbly, acknowledged the woman's flattering comments.

The lady's eyes swept a little enviously over Beth's elegant dress and bonnet. "But your dear wife," she simpered, "surely so close to your time. . .is it really very wise of you, my dear, especially in this heat?"

Beth fought back the hot words on her tongue. It would never do for a minister's wife to say, "Stop ogling my husband, madam! He might be the most handsome man in the colony, but he belongs to me. He's mine!"

The sudden wave of possessiveness shook her, and she was immediately ashamed. It was a moment before she could murmur a polite response.

To her relief, William said hastily, but firmly, "Just so, madam, and I must not keep my wife standing any longer," before bowing again and continuing slowly over to where they had been forced to leave their horse and cart some distance away in the shade of some tall gum trees.

She waited tensely for him to comment on her furious out-burst. But there were still too many people around, and she realized as he nodded or called out cheerful greetings to all and sundry, this was not the time to renew her attack.

After the silence between them had grown too long, Beth sought a little frantically for a topic of conversation and then blurted out, "I wonder if Kate and Adam have met up with John Martin yet."

The arm under her hand stiffened. She glanced up at him, and her heart dropped. Once again that steely look of reserve had settled on his face.

"It is extremely unlikely," he said abruptly. "Adam said even if all went well, the journey would take several weeks, and then it would depend upon where Martin was on the vast property."

"Oh, yes, of course," she murmured swiftly. Recovering quickly she tried again. "Such a shame they missed out on your first formal duty as a minister here in this new colony. I do declare your wedding services get better with each one."

"Thank you, Beth." To her relief, although his tenseness did not disappear completely, he smiled briefly, and then paused as he raised his hat in response to a greeting from a couple who had traveled out on the *Royal Duke* with them from England.

"No word yet from your sister and Mr. Stevens?" one of the women asked. Beth held her breath for a moment and stole a swift glance at William as the stupid woman rattled on. "Such a brave young couple, traveling all that way through the wilderness to Mr. Stevens's station in New South Wales, when only explorers and a few intrepid souls have been all that way overland from here before," she gushed.

"Yes, it was very unfortunate our captain on the *Royal Duke* refused to continue our journey to its completion in Sydney," William responded stiffly. "However, I doubt very much if they would have arrived yet at Mr. Stevens's sheep property."

Beth glanced at him. And that was something else that

puzzled and amazed her. Why did he hate talking about Kate's determination to find John Martin? Why had he refused to discuss any of that with her?

Ever since Adam Stevens and Kate's amazing disclosures about John Martin, William had always cut her off abruptly when she had wanted to discuss it all with him, stating that Lord Farnley's supposed son by a previously unknown marriage to a Spanish woman during the Napoleonic Wars had nothing to do with him. Which, of course, was patently untrue.

Beside the whole business being the catalyst that brought them from England to this new colony, the death of Beth's stepfather had led to them both inheriting a surprising amount of money from his estate. William's forethought in bringing sufficient funds with them so they could purchase property had been most fortunate.

Neither of them had realized just how wealthy his lordship had been, and his nephew Sir Percival Farnley, who for many years had thought himself heir to the title and entailed estate, had been furious at not being left more money in the will, and of course even more furious when the existence of another claimant to his inheritance had been discovered.

Beth's mind snapped back to the present and the persistent woman who had traveled with them on the *Royal Duke*. Somehow Beth managed to smile, to respond appropriately, ignoring the avid curiosity in the woman's eyes as she glanced from Beth to William and back. William murmured the appropriate responses politely, and suddenly Beth wanted to kick him, to scream, to do something that would stop him from treating her as formally as he did everyone else.

Always he was so polite, so correct in his address to her. Just as he was now to these people who were practically strangers. She was his wife, the mother of his children. But sometimes she wondered if they were still even friends.

In the past, only at night in the privacy of their bedroom had something of the old, loving, lighthearted boy she had grown up with returned. But to her increasing pain and bewilderment, even those delightful times together had not occurred for many months now, not since Lord Farnley's funeral and Adam Stevens's intrusion into their lives.

In fact, she thought wearily as she leaned heavily on William's arm, *the last two years has been nothing but turmoil. First, I lost William's constant presence and support, then there was Mother's illness, my foolish friendship with John, and the grimness of our wedding day when it should have been so happy.*

Suddenly Beth felt drained of energy. Her mother had died only a few weeks after the wedding, and there had been no chance of getting used to married life before the early discomforts of being with child had prostrated her.

Then had come the discovery of John Martin's arrest for murder and the dreadful day he had been sentenced. Transportation to Australia for life. She had never really believed her charming young friend could possibly have done such a foul deed.

That horrible period had at the time seemed endless. Even the wonder and delight of becoming a mother had been tarnished. Harold had arrived weeks early. The constant, special care of such a tiny baby had consumed so much of her time there had been hardly a chance to prove to William and his new congregation she could be a good minister's wife, be of some use to him in his onerous tasks as a clergyman.

As though all that had not been enough, Lord Farnley had collapsed. There had been the hasty, long journey back to Fleet-wood from London, and then the very day of his funeral, Adam Stevens had arrived with his information about John Martin.

There was so much about her friendship with John that she had never mentioned to a soul, not even Kate. And certainly she had been too ashamed to breathe a word to William

Perhaps if he had not been so changed, perhaps if he had not shown such determined lack of inclination to talk about John Martin and the whole sad business, she might have plucked up the courage. But as it was, she had been so fearful that he was already disappointed in his wife, in her lack of ability to help him in that parish in London with the impoverished people he had been trying so hard to care for both physically and spiritually.

The muscle in her back suddenly spasmed once more, this time so long and so painfully, Beth held her breath. And then she knew.

"Beth?"

William's sharp, suddenly anxious voice reached her through the wave of pain. She felt his arm go around her waist, and she thankfully leaned on him.

"Oh, dear, oh, dear, is she all right, Reverend Garrett?"

The pain eased, and Beth straightened but stayed close within William's grasp. She started to smile, and then her smile broadened as she saw William's eyes widen in comprehension and then his face go very pale.

"Yes, I'm perfectly all right," she swiftly reassured them both, and then suddenly chuckled mischievously. "Well, as all right as a mother-to-be at this stage can be. But I am afraid I have to ask you to excuse us, madam. We need to make certain arrangements for the imminent arrival of our baby."

A groan burst from William. Before she could protest, he swept her up in his arms and hurried the remaining distance to the cart.

"Why didn't I insist on hiring a proper carriage?" he muttered angrily as he lifted her carefully to the hard, exposed seat.

She had loved being held so close to his strong body, and gurgled happily, "Because there are very few way out—" She stopped abruptly, and her teasing smile disappeared as another, stronger pain swept through her.

William prayed silently all the way home. He should have

known better. He should never have yielded to her reproachful eyes when he had said she should stay safely home. Having her share this first special time after so many barren months not ministering, seeing her delight in having a real occasion for which to dress up and then the delightful prospect of having her all to himself on the journey to and fro had just been too much temptation.

Those few miles along that narrow, bumpy road through the bush were the longest he had ever traveled. Never had he been so glad to see the house come into view. And yet. . .

"I haven't even finished the house properly yet," he muttered grimly, and then hoped Beth had not heard him.

She had, but only gasped, "No matter, I've been prepared for ages. Didn't want to be caught out as with Harold's. . ."

Another pain caught her breath. William glanced swiftly at her, but she was holding her stomach, her eyes closed and her face twisted in pain. He urged the horses to go faster still, but not so fast that he could not avoid the worst bumps to save jolting her around.

So badly he had wanted to build more rooms, but so far there had only been time to finish a couple of bedrooms so they could at least move from the tent on the Youngs' property. All that could be said for their home was that it was dry and kept the rain out! Poor Lucy, so far their only servant, was still sleeping on a cot in the only other room, the detached kitchen.

The pains were coming much faster and stronger. As he hauled on the reins, he started roaring for Lucy to fetch Mrs. Young, praying she would have left the wedding early herself to tend to her own large family.

He was so afraid for Beth, this small woman, still hardly more than a child herself.

"What time I am afraid, I will trust in thee," he quoted over and over, wondering as he prayed through the long hours that followed if the author of that Fifty-sixth Psalm had ever felt like this for someone he loved.

Immense gratitude to a great and merciful God filled William with awe. He stared down at the red, rumpled face of the newborn baby cradled closely to Beth. Tears started to burn the back of his weary eyes. This was his son, flesh of his flesh.

"Would. . .would you like to hold him?"

His eyes lifted to Beth's pale, exhausted face. She was watching him with a curious expression.

"I—" His voice was choked. He swallowed rapidly and tried again. "I didn't mean to disturb you. Mrs. Young insisted you need to rest, but she did say it would be all right to take a peep at you both. I. . .I'm sorry. I just. . ." He drew a deep, much-needed breath.

A gleam of humor flashed into her blue eyes. "You just wanted to see your new son. By the look of you, I think nurses should insist fathers rest also. Do sit down before you fall down, William, my dear."

He only vaguely heard the mild exasperation in her soft voice, but he did sink onto the chair beside her bed, thankful to be off legs that trembled as they had only twice before, when she had been shyly waiting for him that first night and the day when Harold had been born.

Beth lifted the carefully wrapped bundle and handed it to him. "Meet your son, William," she said gently.

Without a word, he stared at her for a moment and then reached out to take her precious gift.

Father. He was a father.

His eyes returned to the sleeping baby. Even as he watched, his son's eyes flickered and opened. The baby's face started to screw up as though to protest being disturbed once again in this crazy new world. One tiny fist slipped out of the covers and waved around aimlessly. William tentatively put out a finger and the tiny fist closed around it. The baby seemed to think better of making a fuss, yawned, and settled to slumber again.

"He. . .he's so tiny," William whispered reverently.

"Not as small as Harold was, but then he is not quite as early," Beth said wearily. "But Mrs. Young did say that with two babies arriving early like this, we had better be extra careful if we have another one. It could be too early and too tiny."

William looked up at Beth sharply, but she was resting back on the pillows again with her eyes closed.

"He looks so much like Harold did," she added softly, and there was no mistaking the satisfaction in her voice.

William stilled. He looked quickly down and studied the tiny scrap, not daring to push the wraps back so he could have a better look. He closed his eyes and clenched his teeth.

Harold.

"Well, don't you agree?" Beth added a little hesitantly after a long moment, and he knew he had let the silence stretch too long.

She was looking at him with a slight frown on her face. He forced a smile and said as lightly as he could, "Well, if you mean all red and scrawny, I'd have to agree."

"William! I'll have you know none of our babies would ever look so horrible! They are beautiful." Beth reached out and gently traced a finger across the tiny cheek still marked by his rough passage into this world. She pushed the cover back from the tiny head, and said proudly, "See, he has just the same mop of black hair Harold did. If anything, it's longer and thicker. And his ears stick out from his head just like yours do."

She was right. He certainly did look like Harold had. William stared and then inwardly sighed. But then, didn't most babies have dark hair and look alike just after they were born?

"Well, he must take after some distant relative, certainly not me or his beautiful fair mother," he said as lightly as he could.

"Oh, I don't know," she said idly, still touching the dark head. "Kate told me once she remembers your hair being a much darker color than it is now."

"She does?" Even he could hear the sharp note in his voice. Beth looked up at him, and he glanced down again and said as casually as he could, "Well, I don't remember ever being as dark as Harold." And then, because he did not think he could take any more comparisons, he added swiftly, "We never did decide on another boy's name if our daughter did not arrive."

Beth's face lightened. She gave an unexpected, unladylike snort. "You may not have thought beyond a daughter's name, but I most certainly have."

He looked up swiftly.

She suddenly smiled at him gently. "We gave Harold my stepfather's name because it pleased him so much and helped lift his sadness after Mother died. This young man shall have his own father's name. But I have always thought that to have the father's name the same only causes confusion in time, so what about James William?"

Beth held her breath, watching William carefully. He had never made any comment about Harold's name, but there had been times she had wondered if he had regretted her choice. And it had been her choice, because he had seemed almost indifferent at the time. In fact, he was already paying more attention to this baby then he ever had to Harold those first few weeks.

To her utter dismay, his eyes filled with moisture, and as she stared at him, one solitary tear made its way down his rough, unshaven cheek.

Deeply shaken and moved, she impulsively touched his hand and murmured, "I love you, William."

His face stilled. A tiny fire blazed deep in his dark eyes so briefly, that afterward she thought she must have imagined it. Then his eyes were hidden as he looked down once more at the baby, before at last smiling gently and reaching for her hand. "And I love you, too, Elizabeth Garrett," he murmured softly.

Beth searched his face and felt a wave of disappointment. Even so had they spoken to each other several times over the years before he had left Fleetwood. It had always been said lightly after some childish prank, his way of letting her know she was forgiven. But this time she could not laugh.

She opened her mouth and then decided this was not the right time—when she still looked so pathetically unattractive and was so exhausted—to tell him the true nature of her love.

His strong fingers closed so tightly around hers she winced. "My father's name was James," he murmured.

She swallowed on the lump in her throat. "Yes, I know," she whispered and felt her own eyes fill with tears of pity for him as they had before when he had first told her why he had come to live at Fleetwood.

Beth knew William could hardly remember his father, cousin to Lord Farnley, who had gone beside her stepfather to fight Napoleon and never returned. His mother had survived until she had instilled in her young son all she could about a personal faith in Christ and then thankfully given him up into the safe guardianship of Harold Farnley before succumbing to a lengthy illness.

Concern for Beth filled William's face. He let her go and stood up quickly. "I was warned not to stay long. You need to sleep. Shall I put. . ." He paused and looked down at the baby in his arms with such a wondering, loving expression on his face that she wanted to reach out and hold them both tightly to her. "Shall I put James William into his crib, or do you want him back on the bed with you?"

"Farva?"

The soft murmur came from the open doorway where a small, tear-streaked face peered through the early morning light. "Harwol come?"

"Harold, what are you doing here?" William's voice was sharp, and the baby in his arms moved abruptly. He lowered his voice and added in a softer voice, "I thought I told you to stay with Lucy until I came to fetch you."

Beth opened her mouth and then closed it abruptly. Several

times during the hours just past, Mrs. Young had assured her William was minding Harold with every care and attention while Lucy had been helping them. But then, he had never failed in kindness to his son, just always seemed to hold himself strangely aloof from him.

"He is trying to say 'Father' and 'Harold,' " she murmured with a teasing smile. "Someone been teaching him, I wonder?"

William actually looked a little sheepish but made a fast recovery. "He is a very bright little fellow, and he was upset at not being allowed near his beloved mother," he replied swiftly.

Her smile widened, but she watched William carefully as he hesitated for a brief moment before looking enquiringly at her. She nodded slightly, and William handed the sleeping baby back to her before going over to the door and swinging Harold up in his arms.

He sat down once more on the chair close to her and put Harold on his knees. "I told you when you woke up we would have a little baby for you. This is your baby brother, and his name is. . .is James William."

His voice cracked slightly, but it was gentle and his face full of understanding of a very small boy's impatience and curiosity as Harold stared with big dark eyes at the small bundle in Beth's arms.

Beth's heart was full. She looked at each face, the man she loved so much, the sleeping baby, and their firstborn who would always hold a special place in her heart. Surely God was good, and as Kate had so many times reminded her through their uncomfortable sea voyage, He would give strength in times of weakness.

It was only a few minutes before William and Harold reluctantly left Beth to her much-needed rest. After the door had closed behind them, she felt happier than she had for a long, long time. Thoughtfully she watched the still gently rocking, small crib William had placed James so gingerly in. He had surprised her with it only a few days before. Apparently he had not been able to buy one and so had spent a lot of time making it himself. At least that explained why she had seen so little of him in the evenings.

Then she frowned slightly. Already he seemed more taken with this baby than he had ever been with Harold when he was as small. Perhaps, like her, he was becoming more used to the idea of being a parent. But then, something about William had changed.

Exhaustion made her close her eyes, but then they flew open. She still did not know why William had behaved so strangely toward her during that wedding service. Somehow, she had to find the right words to ask him without widening the distance between them.

And above all, somehow she had to convince him she truly loved him, had to remove that wall between them until they were truly one forever.

three

Beth surveyed her domain with considerable pride and satisfaction. Once again she marveled at the determination and industry William had exhibited in obtaining the builders and materials to finish their small stone-and-clay house during the six months since James's birth. The last of its extensions was now complete.

Lucy had proved to be an absolute treasure, even if she was so young, but they could still do with more help. Isabel Young gave what advice and help she could, but the running of the household and their little family was Beth's sole responsibility. For someone who had always been surrounded by servants, even in the house in London, she was satisfied they were coping as well as they could in a land where so many things they had taken for granted in the old country were just not available.

Although it still grieved her, that invisible wall between her and William had not seemed as high or unbridgeable since the birth of James. William included both children equally in his cuddles and attention, and these last months Harold had thrived under his father's extra attention.

Somehow, autumn and then the colder days had slipped by so peacefully and busily that she had not dared to mention William's strange behavior at the wedding. As for her own love for him, it continued to be a bittersweet joy mingled with such pain and fear of his rejection that she had never ventured again to tell him.

When the time was right she would tell William that she loved him. As she looked around the cheerful room, a stab of fear touched her. She had prayed so fervently about it all, but still the fear of damaging their fragile new relationship had stopped her. After James's birth when the days became colder, William had determined that they had to let Lucy have her own room instead of the drafty, still-unfinished kitchen. They'd assembled the crib and little Harold's bed in their bedroom, and the four of them had crowded in. But as each month had passed and William had made no move to share his love with Beth, her frustration, disappointment—and then fear—had increased.

Perhaps now. . . She took a deep breath. Perhaps now that the other bedrooms were finished and Harold and James had their own room. . .perhaps now William would pull her close again in the privacy of their room, in their own large bed. As he used to.

She shook off the thought with some difficulty and continued to study the room, looking for ways she could increase its elegance and perhaps help them forget on cozy nights around the fire how different this new life was and how far it was from all that was familiar and comfortable.

She sighed. Despite her efforts, this room was certainly a long, long way from the elegance and space of Fleetwood, or even of the smaller house they had occupied in London with its adequate number of servants. But Beth felt tremendous pride in this home that she and William were creating from nothing in this strange land.

It had taken her long hours, but at last she had finished sewing the curtains and, with Isabel Young's help, had been able to hang them. They certainly added that touch of color needed to brighten up the small drawing room.

She walked across to plump up a matching fat cushion on the couch and then moved over to the fireplace. Using the poker, she stirred up the glowing embers before placing another piece of wood on them. In another few days it would officially be spring. Spring in September. She gave another little sigh. Would she ever get used to this strange upside-down southern land?

Already the days were warming up, but today there had been a chill wind, and the night promised to be very cold. It still seemed strange that winter had come and almost gone without one snowflake. Standing back, she watched as the flames flickered and then began to lap around the timber.

It was a rare, quiet moment. Lucy was in the kitchen, the large room detached from this main part of the building in case, despite all their precautions, the kitchen fire used for cooking somehow got out of control. James was sound asleep, and Isabel had taken Harold with her back to her cottage to play with her own children, assuring Beth that Bessie would keep an eye on him. The two women had become good friends since Isabel had acted as midwife at James's birth.

"Now, my dear," she had admonished Beth before whisking herself and Harold away, "you make sure you rest while you have the chance before James starts making a fuss for his next feed. You are still far too thin and tired. Been going too hard at getting this place to rights, you have," she had scolded gently.

Beth smiled slightly. She knew she was still not quite up to full strength because of a bad cold and nasty cough this past week, and she should really rest as instructed. But she had taken no more then two steps toward the inviting couch when she heard swift steps in the short corridor outside.

"Beth! Are you there, Beth?"

William burst into the room. His face was lit with a smile, instantly dispelling the fears that his urgent tones had aroused. He waved a thick envelope at her.

"Oh, William, is it from Kate?"

The weeks and then the months had slipped by with no word from her half sister. Their original concern about the travelers being able to reach John Martin and give him the good news that his parentage and inheritance had been proven and that their lawyers believed it should be possible for him to have a retrial by his peers at the House of Lords had been superceded by fear that Kate and her party might not have reached their destination safely at all.

"What does she say? Are they in Sydney? When are they returning? Did they find John Martin safe and well?"

William winced inwardly at the last question, but smiled at his wife and said with forced cheerfulness, "I have no more idea then you yet, sweetheart. We can read it together."

He watched the delight flash across her face. She said with a beaming smile, "How just like you not to read it first yourself so we can share it together."

Feeling an instant hypocrite, he hastily said, "It is addressed to us both."

He could not admit to her that he had not read the letter because he was so reluctant to once again be reminded of John Martin's impact on all their lives. The atmosphere between them had not been as tense or distant since James had been born. But then, they had both been so busy, with no real time to spend just on themselves.

He forced a smile at her, pulling her down to sit beside him as he handed her the letter. "Why don't you read it aloud for both of us?" he asked a little huskily, inhaling with delight the delicate perfume that always surrounded her. It reminded him of a fragrant English spring garden in bloom.

She started reading the letter out loud, and then stopped abruptly. He stifled a smile. He should have known she would get carried away and race her eyes over the missive so much faster than reading out loud permitted.

She gave a startled exclamation, and he froze. Then, as his eyes never left her expressive face, he found himself praying fervently. . .praying for her as well as for grace and acceptance for himself.

At last she lifted dazed, wide eyes to his face. "Married!" she burst out. "They are married!"

For a brief moment, his heart stood still, hope raised that John Martin was safely married and even more removed from Beth.

Then reason kicked in. He was not sure about the liberties allowed convicts, even assigned convicts such as Martin, but he did think it unlikely that someone with a life sentence who had served just over twelve months would be permitted to marry. Especially when he lived on a lonely sheep farm—no, station, Adam had called Stevens' Downs—and was unlikely to meet any women, especially one willing to marry a convict.

Beth's eyes had returned to continue scanning the closely written sheets. "They are not going to live way out west on his station, but at some place called Waverley which is only a few days ride west of Sydney! A few days ride. . . !"

Light dawned. "Beth," William interrupted carefully. "Are Kate and Adam married?"

"Yes, yes, and deliriously happy, she claims."

He swallowed a sudden sharp pang of envy and said softly, "I'm so glad for them."

She was still swiftly reading the letter, and a wry smile twisted his lips. From the moment she had first been able to read, she had always become carried away with any missive. How many times in the years he was away from Fleetwood had he pictured her just so devouring the letters he had written to her almost every week. Her replies had been spasmodic, but usually they spilled out a torrent of woes in a young girl's life. Perhaps that was one more reason why her failure to confide in him something so important had eaten into him so deeply.

"If you have finished with that first sheet, do you think I could now peruse it?" he murmured gently.

"Hmm. . ." She absently passed the beginning of the letter to him, still muttering occasionally with surprise. Then, before he had a chance to read more than the first few lines, she gave another sharp exclamation.

Her hand closed convulsively, the page in her hand rustling as it closed around it. She stared up at him again. This time her eyes were filled with horror. Even as he reached urgently to enfold her in his arms, her eyes filled with tears that slowly started down her face.

"What is it? Is it. . .is it John Martin?"

He gathered her closely to him. She put her head against his chest and gave a sob. He relaxed slightly as she shook her head, but then tensed again as she said sadly, "No, no. It's Cousin Percival."

"Percival Farnley?"

"Yes. He. . .he. . .Kate says he's dead."

"Dead! But how. . .? I know they were afraid he meant harm to John Martin ever since they discovered he had left England before us. That was why, when we could not be sure when a ship might arrive, they had to travel overland to warn him, but—"

"He tried to kill them—John, Adam, even Kate. Oh, how dreadful it must have been. She. . .she says he was completely crazed. But. . .but they escaped with help from some aboriginals. Then Percy was thrown by his horse, and they believe he died from snakebite."

Beth pulled away and handed him the letter. "I am afraid you have married into a scandalous family, William," she added with another sob.

Swiftly he read the letter, and then slowly looked up at Beth. In a strangled voice William said, "He was the murderer. Percival murdered your father's gamekeeper and then framed John Martin. He. . .Martin. . .has been completely exonerated and plans to return to Fleetwood to claim it and the title."

She was staring off into space. He wasn't even sure she had heard him. A lace handkerchief was being folded and unfolded by her trembling fingers. There was a faraway look on her face, as though she had gone away from him in her spirit.

"That's why he was there," she whispered. "Why he was smiling just so, pleased. . ."

"Why who was where?" Her words barely registered, and he hardly knew what he had said himself. He was furious with her. Why could she not forget the man?

The anger that seemed to have been churning deep within him for a long time suddenly surfaced out of control. "So your old friend is innocent. In fact, according to Kate he will soon be Lord Farnley!" he snarled.

She jumped at his loud, angry voice and gaped at him. "My. . .my old friend?" she faltered.

Beth stared at William. His face was transformed, a sneer twisting his lips, and his eyes. . . She had never seen such fury in anyone's face before.

"Or should I have said your old *lover* will soon be Lord Farnley?"

"William!"

She sat frozen, staring at him in horror. He knew. Knew about John.

"Lover?"

Surely that was taking it too far though? Her mouth was dry. She moistened her lips and at last said in a strained, dazed voice, "You. . . you know? How. . .what. . .how do you know?"

"I've always known," he snapped coldly. "Despite all your attempts at appearing so innocent, I've always known."

She shrank back. Utter astonishment and pain flooded through her. Never before had William spoken to her as though he hated her.

Even while she craved for him to love her in that special way a man should love his wife, always she had thought of him as a man who loved. He loved God, loved his family, his friends, even loved the unlovely she had seen others shrink from. Whenever she thought of God's love for her, she had always thought it must be a marvelous love, a love beyond description if it was greater than William's love and tenderness for those around him.

Then he closed his eyes tightly. While she was still trying to find her voice, trying to find the right words to answer this new William, he passed his hand over his face and looked at her. The anger had gone, but the dreadful sadness in them was even worse. Something in her heart broke there and then.

"Oh, William," she managed to whisper at last, "I'm sorry, sorry for being so stupid, but I was so lonely, unhappy."

He raised his hand and she stopped abruptly. "There is no need to apologize," he said hoarsely. "With God's help I forgave you a long time ago." He stopped and swallowed. After a moment he muttered, "Or at least I thought I had."

She could not bear the anguish in his face any longer. Springing to her feet she made for the door, anxious to escape so she could give way to the tears starting to well up in her throat. His hand shot out and halted her. She winced, and the grip on her arm loosened slightly.

"Don't go, Beth. Please. I have to know what you are going to do."

The urgency in his voice brought her head up. She swallowed, desperately fighting for control. "Do?" she said in a stifled, confused voice. "Do about what?"

He gave her arm an impatient little shake. "Please, Beth, I have to know what you are going to do about Harold," he said rapidly. "Are you going to tell him?"

Utter astonishment filled Beth. She stared at him blankly. "Tell who what? Harold? And what has Harold to do with this?"

It was as though he had not heard her. His face was dead-white and he continued speaking in such an agonized voice that her confusion and wonderment grew.

"I fought hard to stop myself from loving him, but he is a wonderful little chap. He's twined himself so deeply around my heart I can never give him up. Never. He—" William broke off as a commotion erupted somewhere in the house.

In the kitchen, Lucy's voice screamed. A door slammed, and then light, running feet headed nearer. Simultaneously, Beth and William started toward the door, but before they reached it Mrs. Young's oldest daughter had flung it open and stood holding onto the doorpost, desperately fighting for breath.

Instant terror filled Beth. "Bessie! What is it? Is it. . . Harold?"

She nodded and gasped, "Mother said. . .come quick."

Beth was halfway along the narrow, mile-long track to their neighbor's property before she realized William was just behind her. She stumbled, and his hand steadied her. "Careful, Beth," he cautioned. "Hurting yourself will not help."

Isabel Young ran to meet them. Her white, tear-streaked face brought a moan past Beth's lips.

"Where is he?" William snapped.

"I. . .oh, that's the trouble. I don't know," Mrs. Young panted in a harsh whisper.

"You don't know!" Beth stared frantically around, searching for the little body she had been sure must be lying ill or injured, or. . .or even worse.

"Oh, Reverend Garrett, Beth, I'm so sorry. Bessie says she only turned her back for a moment, and he was gone. We've been out looking for him this past fifteen minutes or more, and there's just no sign of him. I sent her on to fetch you while I came to see if he had returned here."

"Gone! What do you mean, gone?" William's voice was sharp.

Beth took a step forward, but William's strong clasp on her hand tightened. She looked frantically around. Whereas they had money to employ builders, the Youngs were forced to do their own work, and so their house was still only half built in a clearing in the bush. Their temporary home, still the tent lent to them by the emigration commissioner, was a little distance away, surrounded by crates containing their belongings, waiting to go into their new house.

"Where was he last?" William asked sharply, his voice hoarse.

Mrs. Young pointed with a trembling hand to the far side of the clearing. "They. . .they were gathering some sticks for the fire. Bessie says she told him to wait while she went in a little farther to get a big branch that was on the ground, but when she returned he was gone. She swears she could not have been out of his sight and was only gone a couple minutes. At first she thought he was just playing hide-and-seek," the poor woman faltered guiltily.

"She left him alone?" Beth's voice rose hysterically. She had heard dreadful stories on board ship of people lost in the wild Australian bush. And a small child lost. . .their child. . . Harold. . .

"Steady, Beth!" William's arm went around her shoulders, holding her. "You've gone right into the bush there?"

Isabel nodded wearily. "We've called and searched all around until we decided we needed more help. Lizzie is still out searching. Robert left this morning to get more building supplies, but he is due home any moment."

Tight-lipped, William removed his arm from Beth and strode forward. "Show us where you've already searched," he called back over his shoulder.

Oh, God, this can't be happening, he prayed as they spread out and moved swiftly through the bush, calling out, searching desperately, knowing it was late afternoon already and in a few hours would be dark and freezing cold.

I know I've found it so hard not to love him too much, but please, give me another chance to hold him, to love him unconditionally no matter what pain may be mine eventually, he prayed.

Beth felt as though this must be a nightmare from which she would wake up any moment. She plunged recklessly through the bush, not feeling the branches that whipped her face, her legs. She searched and searched, screaming out her child's name until her voice was hoarse. No little voice answered.

William's voice, some distance away, kept roaring out Harold's name long after her own gave out. Her heart was pounding, her breath coming in short gasps. Time had begun to blur. She had no idea how long they had been searching when she stumbled against the root of a tree and paused, leaning her hand against rough bark, trying to catch her breath.

There was a rustle in the short grass near her feet.

She gave a small scream and jumped back. A thick, striped lizard over a foot long scuttled a few feet away. It stopped, on full alert, as it surveyed the intruder. A blue tongue flickered in and out, and she relaxed slightly.

There had been a similar lizard around their own yard, and they had been warned it's powerful jaws could inflict a vice-like painful bite, but usually it did not break the skin unless lacerations were caused when it was forcibly made to let go. She shuddered and gave it a wide berth, moving swiftly on, but now eyeing the ground more carefully as the shadows deepened.

Memory of Percival's fate made her trembling increase. There were far more dangerous reptiles than lizards here. And Harold was such a little boy.

"Oh, my son," she moaned out loud, "where are you?"

She knew men and women from the immediate district had joined the search, but now she could no longer hear their voices. Sunset was fast approaching. Soon it would be dark, cold.

"Harold," she forced past dry lips once more, and then stood still, holding her breath, listening, praying, hoping to hear his lisping little voice call out "Muvva."

Only the noises of the bush answered her. A breeze had sprung up, softly whispering through the branches of the short scrub. A magpie warbled, and then there was silence.

She took another step forward and then paused. Surely the breeze would not make the branches of that thick bush wave like that. Even as she started forward, the branches parted and a dark-skinned figure stepped forward.

Beth froze, ready to flee. Stories had started to circulate through the colony about aboriginals harassing settlers living in the bush on the outskirts of the settled areas. Then, as the aboriginal pushed past the bush in her way, Beth realized it was a woman. There was a movement behind the aboriginal, and a small, frightened little dark face peered out from behind her.

The woman was naked except for a tattered, dirty skirt that hung almost to the ground. Obviously she had been in contact with white people who had been generous with their cast-off clothes, or she had stolen the skirt from some poor woman's clothesline.

The aboriginal gestured and said something in her guttural language.

"I. . .I'm sorry, I don't understand," Beth whispered.

She took a step forward. The woman tensed, looking as though she would flee. Beth stopped. "Please," she said in a louder voice. "My son, he's lost."

The two mothers from such different cultures stared at each other for a long moment.

Beth tried again. She pointed to herself and then rocked her arms, pantomiming the cradling of a baby. The small child ventured once again from behind his mother. He was about the same size as Harold. Beth pointed to him and then to her own chest again.

"My baby, my son," she said desperately, "lost." Tears started to trickle down her cheeks.

The woman's face softened. She hesitated, still watchful, then she shrugged and gestured to Beth to come closer. "Kawai!" she said in a demanding voice. Without waiting to see if Beth obeyed, she turned and made off amongst the trees.

Should she follow? As Beth was desperately trying to make up her mind, she heard a distant shout. This time it was her own name being called. William sounded angry, frightened.

She opened her mouth to answer him, but the strange woman had paused and turned back. She said something softly, then put her hand over her mouth and shook her head.

Suddenly she held her thin brown arms across her chest and rocked them as Beth had done.

Hope leaped into Beth's heart, and she started after her. The woman turned and loped off through the trees again. Beth followed swiftly, feeling clumsy as she stumbled where the woman glided so fast over the ground in her bare feet.

A few minutes later the woman stopped and pointed. Very breathless, Beth came up to her, peering anxiously ahead.

"Wakowako," the woman said abruptly. A flow of other words followed, but Beth had rushed forward toward the small figure lying so still on the ground.

"Harold! Oh, darling!"

Kneeling down she examined him swiftly. There was a cut on his forehead, and blood had trickled down over his eyes. He did not stir as she anxiously picked him up and cradled him in her arms.

The woman spoke again, this time very slowly and hesitantly, "Wakowako. . .child. . .head." She pointed, and Beth saw an exposed root and then the rock with a slight smear of blood on it.

"Thank you, oh, thank you," she managed, despite the tears streaming down her face.

The woman flashed a smile and then shrugged and turned away, gesturing to her own wide-eyed child to follow her.

"Wait," Beth called. "Please wait."

The woman stopped and tilted her head inquiringly.

Beth looked desperately around her. She had no idea where she was, having lost all sense of direction. Suddenly she realized why William had been calling her. She had been crazy blundering off the way she had. Now, she too was lost, and she had the added burden of carrying her small, unconscious son.

four

Beth followed the aboriginal woman, trusting her for some reason she found it hard to explain later to William. When she at last recognized a familiar old, gnarled gum tree, she was totally exhausted and could only gasp silently with relief.

The woman stopped and pointed in the direction of their new home. Beth nodded, too breathless and exhausted to respond or wonder how the woman knew. The aboriginal shrugged and turned to start back the way they had come.

Beth made a tremendous effort and gasped, "Thank. . .you. . ." But the woman simply vanished as silently as she had appeared, her own small boy taking one last, long look at Harold before obeying his mother's sharp command and running after her. The bush swallowed them up, and they were gone.

Gasping for breath, Beth forced one foot after the other. The precious burden in her arms must not be dropped. She was nearly there. She turned the last bend. A baby was crying.

With James in her arms, Lucy was pacing back and forth outside the front door, anxiously peering up the track toward the Youngs'. She saw Beth. A relieved look swept over her face, and she ran toward Beth, James crying even harder.

Beth felt numb. She didn't even feel remorse that her baby was so distressed, no doubt from hunger. Faintness swept through her. She must have swayed, for Lucy made a distressed sound as she reached them and said, "Oh, Miz Garrett, do put him down before you fall down."

Then Beth was sitting on the hard ground, muscles aching, fighting for breath, fighting her whirling head. Vaguely she knew Lucy put James down on the grass near her and took Harold from her vicelike grasp just as she fell back.

"Is he. . .is he. . .?" Lucy's fearful words stopped suddenly.

In a relieved voice she added, "Why, he was only asleep. Look, he's waking up."

With a tremendous effort, Beth lifted her head. She knew it had been more than mere sleep.

A small voice started to murmur, "Muvva? Farva? Where my Muvva?"

"Here. . .darling," she managed to gasp thankfully. "Mother's here." She struggled to sit up, but when she had managed to do so and had pushed away the persistent, descending haze for a moment, she saw he was still again.

William. She needed him. Everything would be all right when William came.

"Get. . .William. . ." she managed to say with another spurt of energy, and then the haze gave way to blackness.

ॐ

Never had William known such fear. He frantically pushed through the bush in the direction he had last heard Beth cry out Harold's name in that hoarse, frantic voice. Several times he had called her after he had realized far too much time had passed since they had made voice contact with each other.

He paused, called her name again, and then waited in breathless stillness for any sound that would indicate where she was. His short, rasping breaths seemed to keep pace with the silent plea flowing constantly from him. *Please, God. Please, God. Keep them safe. Help me find them.*

A feeling of helplessness filled him. Harold lost. Now Beth. What to do? Which way to go?

Slowly his breathing eased, and suddenly he had an overwhelming need to kneel in the dirt. As he fell to the ground, it was as though his whole being swept out in search of the Lord he had committed his will and his life to, his lips putting into hoarse words what had been tormenting his soul since Bessie had interrupted them.

"Oh, Father, I thought in my arrogance that I was so noble forgiving Beth, marrying her, not saying a word of condemnation to her for pretending Harold is my son," he gasped out loud, "but it was still all there in my heart. I have harbored it there. Forgive me my angry words to her. They. . .they showed me my sinful heart. Please forgive. . .forgive me."

He was silent for a moment, and then in a torrent of words he added, "Your Word says love is kind, does not envy, does not boast, is not proud, is not rude, is not self-seeking, is not. . . is not easily angered, keeps no record of wrongs. . .

"Oh, Father, I've fallen so short of all those things, and yet I claim to love her, to love You. Forgive. . ." He groaned in an agony of spirit. "You are faithful and just. Your Word says You have promised to forgive my sins if I confess them.

"Oh, Father, I shouted at her, was so angry, so unkind, and now she is lost and hurting, and I have not told her how sorry I am, how much I love her! Oh, Father, please forgive me. Cleanse me from all unrighteousness as You promised. I want to love as You love. Perhaps then I can someday be of some value to You again in the ministry I believed You called me to."

He fell silent. Gradually his shuddering, his groaning eased. A breeze sprang up. Slowly increasing in strength, it tossed the branches over his head to and fro. It was cold against the wetness on his cheeks, and at last he stirred and opened his eyes. For a moment he thought someone was beside him. He glanced swiftly around, but no one was there. Still, a sense of peace swept over him.

Raising his head, he stared heavenward and sighed. "Thank You, Lord," he whispered humbly.

A few moments later he was on his feet and with a strangely lighter heart started back through the bush in the direction from which he had come. Nothing had changed. Harold and now Beth were still missing, but his panic and fear were gone. God was in control.

A distant clanging noise echoed faintly through the trees. He caught his breath and began to run. It was the prearranged signal Robert Young had devised to announce if a searcher found any trace of Harold.

To William's surprise, he suddenly burst out of the bush onto the track between the two properties. For a moment he hesitated. He was closer to home than the Youngs'. Some impulse made him turn and head away from the clamor of someone hitting a pipe against the old metal bucket Robert had stuck up on a post.

And then he saw them. The three most precious people in his life lying on the ground near the house. His heart stopped. Then he heard the angry, healthy wail of a baby. Beth moved. She started to sit up, and then he was beside her.

"It's all right, Beth. I'm here." His arm went around her, his eyes swiftly searching from one precious face to the other, ensuring they were safe, determining what injuries there were.

"William." There was utter relief in her harsh whisper. She relaxed against him for a moment, and then she stiffened. "Harold. . .is he. . .?" An increasing edge of hysteria colored her voice, and he quickly soothed her.

"He's fine," he assured her automatically, but it was not until he had released her and reached out to touch the filthy, blood-stained little face with his trembling hand that he knew for sure that Harold was indeed fine. The little boy stirred and opened his eyes. He blinked and then focused on him.

"Farva," he said faintly. As William reached to gather the precious little body into his arms, big tears filled the dark brown eyes. His little hand went up to his head. "Hurts, Farva."

Overwhelming love and thankfulness filled William. With his eyes closed tightly to stop his own tears from falling, he gently hugged the slight body. "Poor Harold," he soothed lovingly. "Did you fall over, Son?"

The little head tucked against his neck nodded slightly.

"And what about Mother, did she fall over too?"

The little head lifted and followed his father's anxious gaze across to Beth. She was watching them both silently. Tears had started to run down her face, making pale channels through the dirt and scratches on her cheeks.

James had fallen silent, but just then he stirred and started to let his indignation at being so long neglected made known again in no uncertain terms. He had kicked his covers off, and his plump little legs and arms pumped the air frantically.

"James crying? Muvva crying? They fall over?"

Before William could answer the anxious little question, there was the sound of pounding feet. As Beth reached out to pick up the baby, several people burst around the bend, Robert Young leading them, closely followed by Lucy. He stopped dead, and then walked swiftly forward as Lucy darted around him to pick up and soothe James.

William stood up and called out swiftly, "All seems well." Relieved smiles replaced anxious frowns as he continued quickly, "A bump on the head, and exhaustion, I think. Beth?"

"Oh, Reverend, I didn't want to leave them," panted Lucy, rocking the baby swiftly, "but she keeled over like, and. . .and insisted I find you."

Beth said faintly, "You are a good girl, Lucy. You did exactly as I asked you to." She looked up at William and said in a stronger voice, "And I did not fall over, just ran out of breath." She took a quivering breath and asked anxiously, "Is Harold really all right? He has a cut on his head and was unconscious when I found him, and. . ."

Isabel Young swiftly examined the small boy, who was still clinging to William. She nodded reassuringly, and Beth relaxed at last.

"Where was he? How did you find him?" a desperate little voice asked.

Beth's smile was forced, but a wave of love for her swept through William as she said reassuringly to young Bessie, "I didn't really find him. We were all looking for him in the wrong directions. I think he must have run across your yard and gone into the bush the opposite place we thought he must have. If she. . .she hadn't fetched me. . ."

She looked toward the bush where the woman had disappeared and said in a wondering voice, "There was an aboriginal woman and her child. She took me to Harold. He. . .he had fallen and hit his head on a rock. Then when I realized I didn't. . ." She gulped and looked pleadingly up at William. "I didn't know which direction was home, so she brought me here."

Exclamations of wonder filled the air. Someone said they had seen a small camp of aboriginals several miles back in the bush near a creek.

Then William said firmly, "We have much to thank her for, but we must get you both—" A slight smile touched his pale face as he raised his voice over James's increasing bellow. "We must get all three of you looked after now."

Eager hands helped Beth to her feet and urged her toward the house. A sudden cheer went up from the other neighbors and friends who had also just arrived on the scene and saw their search was over.

At the bottom steps, William turned and surveyed the small crowd helplessly. What could you say to people like these who had left their urgent tasks so selflessly to help?

"Thank you, every one of you," he called out in a loud voice. He swallowed, and a brief hush descended. Feet shuffled in the dirt. Something suddenly moved him to say, "Tomorrow is the Lord's Day. If any of you would like to return here, perhaps you might like me to lead a church service for you?"

There was dead silence. William stared helplessly from one surprised face to another. Would they be offended? Had he been presumptuous making such an offer?

Several of the men and women looked at each other, and then someone called back eagerly. "You mean that, parson, sir? We haven't been able to get into town to any services for weeks."

William assured them earnestly that he did. "It's the very least I can do for all your help," he added eagerly, "and I can assure you I'll prepare the best sermon I ever have. Not too long, though," he hastened to assure them.

There were a few friendly chuckles, a time was set, and excited chatter marked their departure.

While Beth tried to feed and settle James, William insisted

on bathing Harold himself, despite Lucy's protests. "You go and prepare something for us all to eat," he ordered her firmly.

Knowing Beth would not want to let Harold out of her sight just yet, he dragged the large tub into their bedroom where she was resting on the bed while she attended the baby's needs. He did let Lucy bring hot water from her large kettle, but he gently removed Harold's clothes himself, quickly examining him for any other injuries before lifting him into the soothing water.

"Just a few scratches on his legs and the cut and bump on his head, I think," he hastily reassured Beth.

She nodded briefly and relaxed.

Suddenly there was tension between them. The angry words he had flung at her before Bessie had interrupted hung again in the air. William found himself avoiding her eyes as he dried the now-fretful Harold and then persuaded them both to eat a few mouthfuls of the nourishing supper Lucy brought in. He hesitated only briefly before carrying the small boy over to lie beside Beth.

That was his place, where he should be sleeping every night, but he had been so unsure of his welcome he had not been there for so many long, lonely nights.

"If you prefer, he can sleep near me tonight," he said gruffly, "but I think if he wakes up he will want to see you first."

"And who's fault is that when you spend so little time with him?"

William froze. Slowly he raised his head. There was a decided, militant sparkle in her beautiful blue eyes. She gazed at him steadily. He chose to ignore the condemnation and query in her gaze.

Instead, he said quietly, "I can never tell you how sorry I am for the way I spoke to you before. Please forgive me, Beth."

To his relief her expression softened, but then, to his consternation it hardened again.

"I have absolutely no idea what you were talking about, what you were so angry about, William Garrett. Surely what happened with John. . ." She stopped, an arrested look on her face. "How did you know about him, about my knowing him before?" she demanded.

He hesitated, looked from her to Harold, who at that moment gave an immense yawn and snuggled closer to his mother's warmth.

"We cannot discuss this now," he said curtly, "and I have a service to prepare for tomorrow. Perhaps after everyone has gone we will get a chance to talk."

"We most definitely will," she declared with a trace of anger. "Oh, yes, William, we most definitely will make a chance to talk. Our talk is months—many months—overdue. I have questions, and I expect an answer to every one of them. I need answers, lots of them, and this time nothing is going to stop me from getting them!"

He stared at her blankly for a moment. Beth held his gaze with some difficulty but determined not to look away first. For a moment he looked bewildered, and then to her utter relief, he nodded abruptly and without another word strode from the room.

Exhaustion swiftly claimed Beth, giving her no time to think, to dwell on that strange, angry scene after reading Kate's letter. But it was still dark when Harold woke her up, his little body shaking with sobs.

Alarmed, she turned up the lamp, noting William's bed was empty, but glad he had left the light. Quickly she checked the bandage over the cut on Harold's head, which had proved to be relatively minor, despite the amount of blood that had covered his face and hair. She drew him into her arms, murmuring soothing words, rocking him gently until the crying started to ease at last to a few hiccuped sobs.

"Is he all right?"

She looked up swiftly at the soft whisper. William was standing beside the bed, staring anxiously down at Harold.

"Farva!"

The small boy wriggled strongly. When she let him go, he

flung himself at William, then clung fiercely as his father's strong arms closed around him.

Beth stared at them. "I think you were wrong," she murmured tearfully as Harold at last gave a few more quivering sighs, then relaxed and snuggled against his father's chest as William sat down on the bed beside her, holding him close. "He feels safer with his father."

William gave a shaken laugh that was almost a groan. She knew him well enough to know he was attempting to deliberately lighten the moment when he gave another, much lighter chuckle and said chidingly, "But surely it's the mother's prerogative to get up for the children in the middle of the night, so I hope this does not mean a sign of things to come."

For some inexplicable reason Beth's spirits lifted. "And I most definitely think every son should prefer his father to look after him, especially in the middle of the night," she added swiftly, settling back comfortably onto her pillow.

"Well, fathers—especially ministers of such a high and lofty calling—are the breadwinners," he intoned in pious, lofty tones, "and have many other, far more onerous, serious, er. . .dignified responsibilities and. . .and should not be laughed at by their wives!"

By this time, Beth had succumbed to giggling, suddenly feeling lighthearted, free to tease him for the first time in many, many long days. "Of course, William, most certainly, William," she managed in a worshipful, humble voice, and then spoiled it with another irrepressible giggle.

William's mouth twitched, but he continued in his best pompous voice, intoning softly but mournfully, "Such levity, madam, especially in the minister's wife, is not to be tolerated. She should demonstrate sober piety and good works at all times, especially when it means letting her good husband sleep!"

"What about her bad husband?"

William stared in mock horror at her laughing face. And then he too succumbed and laughed out loud, immediately trying to stifle his deep laugh to a choked gurgle of amusement as the dozing Harold stirred in protest at being disturbed.

"Oh, Beth, you are such a darling woman," he whispered softly, earnestly, and then he was suddenly still, staring at her with an expression on his face that made her catch her breath, driving away her amusement and replacing it with a bewildering array of emotions.

Desperately striving to maintain the good feeling that had sprung up between them so unexpectedly, she murmured back, "Well, Reverend William, to overcome our problem, I think you should share this parenting and stay with us for the rest of the night."

She swallowed rapidly, fighting the urge to beg him fervently to stay, desperately frightened he would rebuff this tentative reaching out to him.

"So, if Harold wakes up from a nightmare again, you will be there for him of course," she added swiftly and with a catch in her voice at the light that sparkled at her from his suddenly intent eyes.

Without a word, he stood and leaned over her, putting Harold gently down beside her. He murmured a protest, and William's large hand stroked the black curls back from the bandage on his head. To Beth's immense relief he whispered, "It's all right, Son. I'm not going anywhere, I'll be with you . . .with both of you, in just a moment."

Only then did Beth realize he was still dressed in his day clothes and had not been to bed at all. He had been watching over his family. Watching over her. Over Harold.

"William. . ." Her voice choked, but she managed to smile at him.

Something flared in his eyes. He bent down again. "I will be back in a moment," he assured her firmly. With that he hesitated for the briefest moment.

Then she felt his mouth brush her lips gently. Instinctively she moved closer, reaching up for his lips. She heard the soft intake of his quick breath. He gave a muffled groan, and then he was kissing her with a passion, a desperation she had never known. Then it was over, far too quickly. He straightened and was gone.

With a pounding heart, she waited for his return and only relaxed at last with a soft sigh when, after what seemed an eternity he returned, strode around to the other side of the bed, and climbed in beside Harold.

She turned to face him in the wide, four-poster bed that he had built with his own hands. "Thank you, William," she said softly.

A hand reached across Harold. She placed her own in it, and he squeezed it gently. For a long moment he held it in his soft grasp. Then in a husky voice, he whispered back, "Good night, my darling wife," before letting her tingling hand go.

His darling wife.

For a long time, Beth lay staring into the darkness. A slight smile tilted her lips. William had joked with her as he had years ago before their marriage. Not until now had she realized just how badly she had missed the old easy communication between them. Since he had asked her to marry him, there had been something—a reserve in him, perhaps a deep inner fear in her of saying and doing the wrong thing with this new William—that had stopped her from teasing him as she had always taken such delight in doing.

But tonight he had been different somehow. And that despite the strange encounter after reading Kate's letter.

She stopped smiling.

She would not think about that now. William had once again joked with her. He was once again in her bed, even if their child was between them.

Something deep inside her relaxed for the first time since they had left England. At last her eyelids drifted closed. Her heart lifted in a silent prayer of thanks and praise.

Tomorrow they would talk. Tomorrow everything would be beautiful and right.

five

William woke slowly. As exhausted as he had felt, he had not been able to relax while lying so close to Beth, and it had been hours before sheer exhaustion had made him sleep. For a moment he was disoriented. There was a golden cloud in front of his eyes. Some parts of it were brushing his face with soft, silky strands. He brought up his hand to brush it aside, and froze. It was hair. Beth's beautiful, golden hair.

He was where he had so longed to be these last weary months, beside her in their bed.

She was lying facing him, her long eyelashes shielding him from the force of her sky blue eyes. Her long hair had not been confined in its usual nightcap and was drifting in glorious confusion over the bedclothes. He reached out toward her and then stilled.

Harold. He was no longer there.

William sat up swiftly and looked around. The door was open, and he relaxed as he heard first Harold's distant, childish voice chattering away in his own mainly incomprehensible language and then Lucy's soft murmur. William's eyes turned to study Beth. She was lying so still, her face mostly hidden by her hair. He could see she was still rather pale, yet a bright pink glowed high on her cheekbones.

It was not often he was able to study her unobserved. A sharp pang went through him at the hollows in her cheeks and the faint line on her forehead. She had been so young when they had been married, barely out of the schoolroom, and was still just twenty years of age. His look intensified, searching for the child who had captured his heart so many years ago with her sad, frightened eyes, who, despite her fears, had tilted her chin and set her lips as though ready to take on whatever unpleasant new future she might have at Fleetwood.

Beth had never been lacking in courage, neither the child nor the woman she now was. Their journey across 15,000 miles of ocean with a small boy and another baby on the way had shown how much courage she possessed. And then, only weeks after their arrival here in South Australia, William had declared his enthusiasm for staying indefinitely in this exciting new settlement where there were still very few clergy to give spiritual guidance and help.

"There were apparently many Christians in the very first company of emigrants, especially on board the *Duke of York*," he remembered telling Beth eagerly. "By some reports it was almost a floating church and Sunday school. But most leadership has been from laypeople, not ordained ministers.

"Divine services have been held regularly right from the day of the first arrivals, even before the governor arrived. I've talked with the appointed colonial chaplain, Reverend Howard. He told me he used a sail to erect a tent in Adelaide for the very first needs of the church. And despite all the other pressing requirements of the colony, the foundations of Trinity Church were laid within days of our own arrival."

William had paused for breath. Beth had been smiling gently at him, but there had been no mistaking her intense interest, and he had gone on to tell her that there was much for a minister of the gospel to do in this new land. He had heard of several other groups of Christians of various persuasions meeting together without shepherds.

"Oh, Beth," he had enthused, "there is a spiritual hunger here, so many sheep without a shepherd, and I believe this may be where God would have us serve Him."

Beth had tilted her head thoughtfully, studying him with an expression he could not quite fathom. Then she said quietly, "I agree, there is much to do here for God, and if that is what you believe God wants us to do, it will be fine with me."

He had loved her even more then. But still, he had not dared to tell her that the circumstances surrounding their marriage had played havoc with his effectiveness as a minister at the church in London. He had known it, and the church authorities there had seemed almost relieved when he had resigned. But now, his old zeal and love for preaching the Word and serving God and the church had returned, as well as a burning desire to tell all who would listen of God's love that caused Him to send His salvation, His joy, in His Son, Jesus Christ.

So William had swallowed, longing to draw Beth into his arms and kiss her senseless. Instead, he had been so stupid. She had been bearing his child, he had told himself, and it was not the time. Like an idiot he had just smiled and moved quickly away before he had yielded to the temptation of taking her into his arms, plundering her soft, red lips. Having that wedding to perform not long afterward had weakened him even further.

Now he feasted his eyes on her. She was more beautiful than she had ever been, had matured into the most beautiful woman he had ever seen. No wonder other men appreciated her beauty, her charm.

He closed his eyes tightly. *Lord, teach me to love until there is no envy.*

Without looking again at the tempting vision, he carefully rose so as not to disturb her slumber. He had work to do. Besides, it was unfair to cause her more stress on top of yesterday. Not daring to look back, he hastened from the room.

To his dismay, it was later than he had hoped. After swiftly cleaning and then dressing in his best clerical clothes, there was only time for quick hugs and kisses with Harold and drinking the cup of tea Lucy insisted on pouring for him. Then he shut himself in the small room he had commandeered as a study to finish working on his sermon and service.

❧

For one breathless moment, Beth had thought William might reach out across the bed for her.

He had sat so motionless, and then she had heard the slight rustle of the bedclothes as he had moved. Her eyes had flown open, but he was already on his way to the door, his back stiff and straight. Not once did he look back.

Her mouth had opened to call out to him, but then she remembered it was Sunday and he had the church service to prepare for. Their time was not now. Would it ever be? Her lips tightened. It most certainly would!

Ever since Harold had disturbed her several minutes before by his little hands patting her face and then crawling over her to get out of bed and find Lucy, she had lain there watching William. She doubted he had managed much sleep that night if even Harold had not woken him.

He had been so upset yesterday before Bessie had interrupted them. She had thought about that, trying to fathom what he had been so disturbed about. It had been something in Kate's letter.

With a swift, indrawn breath, a dreadful thought came. But she quickly dismissed it, the sudden fear, the anger, more than she could bear this morning. It was simply impossible William could think such a thing of her. He must have meant something else.

She sighed deeply. She should have called him back. Asked him.

Disappointment swept through her in waves, followed by anger and disgust at her cowardice in closing her eyes the moment he had stirred and leaving them closed, hoping, praying he would lean over and pull her into his arms, kiss her properly.

She should have reached over and kissed him!

She smiled slightly, picturing his surprise, and suddenly wondered how he would have responded. Her smile disappeared and she shivered. She would not have been able to stand it if he had repulsed her.

With another weary sigh, she climbed out of bed, wincing at stiff, overused muscles from the day before. The cuts and scratches on her legs felt very sore, and she knew she should have attended to them more last night than simply giving them that quick wash. One cut looked very red around the edges, and with a sigh, she washed the dried blood away again, wrapping a makeshift bandage around it. There was no time to fuss over her aches and pains. There was much to be done before the service.

Suddenly she wished William had not invited all those people here today, and still more, that Lucy and Mrs. Young had not suggested it would be a nice gesture to give everyone a picnic lunch after the service.

More delay in having their talk.

Harold, with the resilience of a small child, had recovered from his adventure, despite the bruise and cut on his forehead. When she had finished dressing and walked into the kitchen, he greeted his mother with a beaming smile, while he continued playing with the piece of dough Lucy had given him.

Beth bent down swiftly to hug him and plant a kiss on his sticky face. She removed the now gray lump despite his protests and cleaned his hands on a damp cloth. Sitting him on her knee, she looked him steadily in the face and said in her sternest voice, "Harold, you must never, never go by yourself into the bush like you did yesterday. Not ever again."

He stared at her, and then his bottom lip quivered.

Her voice softening, she added quickly, "Mother and Father could not find you, and we were very frightened." Her hand went out and touched the fresh bandage on his head. "You were all alone when you hurt yourself." A shudder shook her at what could have happened if the aboriginal woman had not found him, and she hugged him tightly.

Harold pulled away and smiled a little tentatively at her. "Harwol not alone."

Beth hesitated. Just how much did a little boy not yet three understand? "Bessie told you to wait for her. When you ran away by yourself you were alone. You must never do that again."

His face lit up and he shook his head vigorously. "Not alone. Black boy ver."

She stilled. Taking a deep breath, she asked carefully, "You went with the black boy, the aboriginal?"

His head went up and down. "Nice boy. We play runnin' an' hidin'."

Beth moistened her lips and then asked softly, "Was his mother there too?"

He dropped his eyes and kicked his legs to and fro without answering her.

"Harold?"

He shook his head slowly and then peeped up at her. "His Muvva come an' ver', ver' cwoss. She. . .she not nice. She yelled at us. I wunned away, and she chased me."

Beth drew in a swift breath. He must have run after the little aboriginal boy, and his mother had found them. Perhaps she had even been nearby or close enough when they had been calling out Harold's name. Perhaps she had been worried what the men would do to them if they thought her son had enticed Harold into the bush. No wonder she had not wanted Beth to call out to William.

"Oooh, Miz Garrett, that awful aboriginal made him get lost!"

She had forgotten Lucy. "Lucy, that woman probably saved his life," she snapped. "She could have just left him there and not bothered to find me."

Harold's little body tensed. Taking a deep breath, she said quietly, "I think her son must have been as naughty as Harold. Perhaps he had even run off from her to watch the children at the Youngs' place. We wondered how Harold could have been where he was, thought he must have run around in a big circle through the scrub."

Beth paused and then added thoughtfully, "But he must have run right across the clearing from where they were looking for kindling and raced into the bush there after the other boy. No wonder Bessie could not find him, why he disappeared so quickly."

After a moment, she added, "The boy's mother must have

found them some time later and yelled like many mothers would. Perhaps she had been frightened because her son had disappeared too. I suspect Harold ran off and she tried to stop him, but he tripped and hit his head."

Lucy, her eyes wide, opened her mouth, but Beth said with a glare, "I am so thankful the woman didn't just desert him and run off, and I do not want you to say a word to anyone about this, anyone, do you hear? I'll tell Reverend Garrett myself after the service. I'm sure we have nothing to worry about with that woman."

Lucy nodded reluctantly, but said, "I've heard some dreadful things about what aboriginals have done, been really big nuisances to settlers like us away some from Adelaide. But now we have a new police force—"

"And I've heard some dreadful things done by whites to aboriginals," Beth interrupted swiftly. She shook her head at Lucy, glancing significantly at the big-eyed Harold. "Now, no more of this. We have too much to do for this picnic after the service."

Beth helped as much as she could, mixing the flour to make dough for the bush dampers and peeling more vegetables given to them by the Youngs. But eventually she had to attend to James's needs and dress both children and herself in their best Sunday clothes, leaving Lucy to place the dampers to cook in the hot coals of the fireplace and finish adding the vegetables to the huge pot of soup already hanging over the fire.

By midmorning, Beth was feeling very weary and was still stiff and sore. When William joined her to welcome the early arrivals for the church service, he also looked pale and drained.

Only a few families gathered together, but because they would not fit in the house, they sat on improvised seats or sprawled on the grass or ground near the house. There was no cold breeze as there had been the day before. A perfectly clear blue sky shone on them, and before the service commenced, several even sought the shade of the tall gum trees nearby.

William felt more nervous than he had since the first service at which he had ever led and preached. For far too long before that wedding service the day James had been born, he had dreaded getting up and preaching. But God had dealt with him that day, given him a passion for sharing the Word. Certainly there had been times of talking about spiritual things to different folk at various times. However, there had been no opportunity to lead a service since that day, let alone be responsible for the sermon.

And to his deep regret, there had been so little time to prepare this one. Last night he had found some old sermon notes and started going over them. But they had not been about what was on his heart, so he had quickly roughed out notes for a completely new sermon, spending as much time in prayer over it as he could. Despite scant sleep, William felt invigorated, eager to preach for the first time in many long months.

And the Lord's presence seemed so wondrously close all through the service. To the unexpected accompaniment of Robert Young's small concertina, they sang a few old hymns with gusto. He heard Beth's pure soprano voice soaring with the others and, catching her gaze, beamed at her. His gaze traveled to their two sons. James was in her arms, and he was pleased to see she had let Bessie sit beside her to help look after Harold.

His gaze kept wandering back to the precious small boy, and when he led them in prayer, it seemed as if all creation held its breath as his fervent words of thanks and praise for God's protection the day before soared heavenward. When he finished, there was a murmur of earnest "Amens." The women, including Beth, had to resort to using handkerchiefs, while there was considerable self-conscious clearing of throats by some of the men.

Then, even William felt the added fervor and conviction in his voice as he preached about God's gift of His only beloved Son, who had willingly died on a cruel cross for each one of them. He spoke wonderingly of the Father's faithfulness, His providence and loving care, His desire to have constant fellowship, unbroken by sin, with those He loved.

Only then did the forceful words waver, his voice soften in awe, as he described God's wondrous grace, His willingness to forgive His children's sin that would keep them separated from enjoying the reality of the love He filled them with, making it possible for them to love each other as He wanted them to.

Beth listened in awestruck stillness. Never had she heard William preach like this. A deep yearning began somewhere deep within her to know God even a little like William spoke of him.

The message was couched in simple, understandable words. At the wedding she had been so consumed with her own shattering discovery that she had later remembered only a few fragments of the message on the Love Chapter.

William had always preached a good sermon. His learned utterings had always been received well by his congregations, but none had ever listened as intently as this small group of people in the Australian bush.

Beth glanced around at their absorbed faces with pride. And then she was swept up again in the torrent of words, the glow on William's face, his shining conviction that what he was saying was irrefutable truth from the Bible, God's Word.

"God loves me. God loves you. He so loved us, He gave His Son to die for me, for you. Forgiveness is there if we ask. . . We can forgive others only if we are first forgiven. . ."

The reality hit Beth as never before. God could forgive her all her sins, all her stupid mistakes, what she should have done and had not. He loved her not because she had proved herself good enough, worked hard enough to earn His love and forgiveness, but because His very nature was love. She simply needed to accept His free gift of love, of Jesus, of life. She did not have to strive, just believe and receive. . .

After they had sung one final hymn and William had closed in prayer, the women started to bustle around preparing their picnic lunch. The older children, like Bessie Young, kept an extra-close eye on the small children and babies, while the men drifted together, yarning about the different events occurring in the colony.

South Australia's first governor, Sir John Hindmarsh, had sailed for England in July. There was great speculation over who would replace him.

"Just as well Hindmarsh has gone," someone snorted. "He's been a constant source of conflict since the beginning when he disagreed strongly with the surveyor, Colonel Light, about the site for Adelaide. If the colonists had not held that mass meeting and backed up Light, Adelaide may have been built closer to Holdfast Bay."

William thought about the long, hot trek into Adelaide that first day and wondered how it may have been if Hindmarsh had prevailed, but he kept silent. As they had found out, it was certainly a long way from good freshwater, as well as other problems.

"Since then he was far too often in disagreement with the colonization commission," another man contributed. "I know he may be a tough naval officer who fought at the battles of the Nile and Trafalgar, but Hindmarsh should not have begun suspending public officers the way he did."

There were a few murmurs of agreement, but then Robert Young said with a worried frown, "I just hope he is not right about this area not being suitable for our city of Adelaide, though. The biggest problem here is no good source of freshwater. Many of the wells we have sunk are no good. Where water has been found, it is often far too brackish for use. I doubt if the Torrens River is large enough to sustain any large population.

"There are already about 4,000 inhabitants in the place, with more ships arriving every few weeks. But to my way of thinking there will be far too little land under cultivation to feed everyone if we don't watch out. Seems to me too many have been too concerned with putting up buildings and not clearing and planting crops."

There were strong words of agreement, but some argued that the women and children needed a good roof over their heads as their first priority. William knew many of them were already desperately trying to clear their small acreages enough to get crops in. He listened carefully, hoping to understand the pressing concerns of these families he had endeavored to minister to that morning.

Robert added solemnly, "As we all know, the river is very low just now. In fact, I have been told last summer was much drier than the previous two years. Hear tell the drought is very bad throughout New South Wales and right down to Melbourne. Crops and stock losses have already been severe."

William felt a sudden trace of fear for Adam, who had so quickly become a good friend. And Kate—she had said very little about their journey in her letter. Perhaps the drought had made their overland sojourn even more of a hazard than had been expected?

The letter.

But he must not think of that now. He forced himself to listen to the conversations around him. Only as he learned to know and understand these people would he be able to exercise any kind of pastoral care.

"Well, it is a shame the big Murray River is not closer, that's for sure, but if we were any farther west over Gulf Spencer at Port Lincoln where some first thought the capital should be, we'd be even farther away from the rest of the settlements and any help we might need," a grizzled old man was drawling. "Especially now that Charles Bonney and Joseph Hawdon have pioneered the first overland cattle route from Goulburn River, just south of the Murray, to Adelaide."

"What a sight that was!" William managed a genuine smile. "Apparently they only lost four of those long-horned cattle."

"You saw them arrive, Rev?"

With an effort of will, William pushed aside his own problems and smiled inwardly at the casual mode of address. The barriers had certainly come down, thanks mainly to Harold's adventure. This was proving to be a great opportunity to get to know the men in the area. From now on, perhaps the naturally reserved, independent settlers would feel more free to call on him for help in spiritual matters.

He grinned at the eager young man and nodded. "I did ride out and see them—and the few sheep they had, as well. First week in April it was when they arrived. Took them nearly twelve weeks, they reckon. But what a sight was Joseph Hawdon. I happened to be in Adelaide the day he walked in. His filthy cabbage-tree hat had those broad black ribbons I'm sure you've all heard about."

There were a few nods and chuckles.

"He was booted and spurred," William continued, "his stock whip in his hand and a filthy clay pipe in his mouth."

"Well," drawled the older man, "reckon he might 'a' run out of bacca though."

There was a general laugh, which William joined in, although some knew his stand against the smoking of tobacco.

"Well," Robert Young said firmly, "now they've proved it can be done, I am sure we can expect many more animals brought over from the east in ever larger numbers. But my money's on sheep, not cattle."

William ignored the gambling reference and said thoughtfully, "A friend of ours, Adam Stevens, agrees with you. He has thousands of sheep in the outback, hundreds of miles west of Sydney. He thinks sheep seem to suit the drier areas better than cattle."

"That's the friend of your sister-in-law who went overland with her, isn't it?" Robert asked curiously.

William nodded abruptly.

"Brave young couple, brave young couple to—" Robert broke off and suddenly slapped his hand against his thigh.

"That reminds me, William. Meant to tell you yesterday, but in all the excitement. . ." He smiled and then continued lightly, "In Adelaide I happened to mention to someone you had bought the Inghams out. When a bloke heard your name, he said he was sure that was who some man was trying to find.

Reckoned he had just arrived from Sydney aboard a ship that was taking some more supplies on board before continuing on to England. Apparently was most anxious to find you before they leave."

William tensed. "Did they say what he looked like?" he asked sharply.

Robert shook his head. "Sorry, friend, didn't think to ask, but they did say he claimed to be some new lord on his way back to England." He chuckled. "They thought that was a bit of a suspicious tale because he had a slight foreign accent like no real English aristocrat would have. They said it was most strange, because he was certainly dressed like one would expect a lord to dress."

"Please, Reverend Garrett," Lucy's excited voice said behind them. "Miz Garrett said to tell you we was ready to eat, and if you would say the blessing, please."

William silently led the men over to join the women and children. His voice did not quiver as he raised his voice so all could hear and thanked God for providing their food and for those who had worked so hard to prepare it.

A cold wind had sprung up, but it was not the cold that made his hands tremble as Beth approached him with his bowl of soup and some damper. Although his lips had stilled, silently and fervently he was still praying. . .praying for them both, for Harold.

John Martin. He was here.

And now William would have to rely on God's faithfulness to help him meet the man, to help him cope with all that could happen now that John was Lord Farnley, a wealthy man and owner of Fleetwood.

six

The people did not linger long after the picnic lunch. While the September days were lengthening, there were still many chores to be done before night fell. As they said farewell, several expressed their thanks for the church service.

The old grizzled farmer said gruffly, "A right powerful sermon, Reverend, right powerful," before tramping off after his wife and passel of children.

After everyone had gone, Beth turned to her husband and said seriously, "I agree, William, that was without a doubt the best sermon you have ever preached."

He had swung Harold up to sit on his shoulders so he could better see to wave good-bye to the Young family, the last to leave. Somewhat to her surprise, at her words William swung around and stared at her. A touch of color rose into his tanned cheeks, and then he smiled slightly. "But you always have praised my sermons, Beth," he murmured.

"No, I mean it," Beth said earnestly. "Perhaps what happened to Harold yesterday made me realize as never before how much it must have cost God to not just lose His Son, but to give Him up."

She looked away from the intense way William was looking at her. It had never been as easy for her to talk about God as it was for William.

A little hesitantly she said, "There was also something special about having the service here."

She looked up at the towering gums. Several wattle trees were already in golden bloom, their glory beautiful amid the many and varied shades of green foliage. For a moment they were silent, listening to the twittering of the birds.

She smiled suddenly. "Even when that bird, a kookaburra they called it, I think, started laughing in the middle of singing that hymn, it did not jar. It seemed to be fitting somehow—a raucous laugh to be sure, but a happy sound. I love the beautiful cathedrals back home, but here. . . God was so close in a strange kind of way," she burst out, and then dared to glance at him to see if he understood her foolishness.

He was staring thoughtfully at her and was silent for so long, she felt embarrassment steal over her. William's faith in God and his obvious love for the Scriptures and his ministry had always awed her, even made her feel somehow inadequate.

All her life she had been taken to church. It was as much a habit of her everyday week as eating and sleeping. She even said her prayers during the week, but it had never really meant to her what it seemed to mean to William—or her stepsister, Kate, come to that. There was a glow about William sometimes after he had spent time alone in his study, where if she entered quietly, she would often find him on his knees.

She had always admired William's desire to become a minister. It had been obvious to her he believed God had called him into the ministry and that it was not just pious words he had uttered when telling his guardian why he had made his choice of study. When Lord Farnley had at first expressed his disappointment that William had no higher ambitions, Beth had supported William, even though she had secretly never really understood the extent of his passion for the things of God. But after today's sermon, she understood better.

Harold had been quite content to sit on his father's shoulders watching the distant figures, his tiny hands clinging to William's head. A brightly colored parrot suddenly screeched and swooped over their heads. Harold chortled with delight and drummed his heels on William's chest.

William tightened his grip on the little legs to protect himself. "Ouch! Gently, gently, young man!" He pretended to bite at the little ankles and growled like a puppy. Harold squealed with delight. "Your mother is filling my ears with sweet praise, and you kick me. Now what is one to think of that, huh?" he teased, tickling the little legs.

More often than not, Harold managed to discard his little shoes, but this day, due no doubt to Bessie's diligence, they were still on his feet. One suddenly came off in William's hand.

"What's this, what's this, then?" he cried playfully, ripping off the little knitted sock Beth had so carefully made with her own hands, "I think it's someone's foot, Mother! Oh, dear."

He stopped and examined the little foot carefully, and then quickly exposed the other foot also. "Beth," he said, suddenly serious, "these shoes are much too tight. They've left marks. Look," he commanded.

Beth had been enjoying their antics, that secret place inside her rejoicing at the light of love on William's face as he played with his son. The reserve that he had for so long shown with Harold seemed to be now gone completely.

Obediently she came closer and looked. "My, my," she said lightly, "our boy has grown. We need to do some shopping." She stopped and added a little anxiously, "So many things here are hard to find. Do you know anyone who might sell small shoes for little boys?"

William thought for a moment and then smiled cheerfully. "As a matter of fact I think I do. I met a certain William Pedler in town last week. Apparently he arrived with his brother Joseph and their young families aboard the *Royal Admiral* only a couple weeks after we landed at Holdfast Bay."

Beth frowned. "The poor dears. I hope they did not have to spend their first night in South Australia like we did in that place they called a storage shed."

William's smile slipped a little, and she knew he was remembering the anxiety, the fear, that dreadful night. They had just been informed by the captain that he was sorry, but he was not going to risk his ship sailing through Bass Strait between the mainland and Van Dieman's Land because of the reports of heavy seas and more bad storms expected up the east coast to Sydney.

They had thought they would only be disembarking briefly while the ship was repaired and loaded with fresh supplies. Instead, Adam Stevens and William had had to supervise the unloading of all Adam's cargo as well as their baggage. Longboats had taken them from the ship to as close as they could get to the beach. Despite their protests, all the passengers' belongings and cargo from the ship had been dumped in a huge heap on the fine, white sand just above the high-water mark and left to their owners to find and sort out.

One of the crew had carried Harold from the boat, while William had been so tender, so carefully holding her, as he had waded through the shallow water to the sand. Not trusting her to any other arms, she had fancifully thought. His concern for her had eased some of her hurt of his avoidance of her during the journey, but afterward, his reserve had returned more than ever. One day she had bitterly decided that he had just been concerned that no harm would come to their unborn child. Perhaps unfairly, she admitted now.

Never over all the years had she been able to fault William's protection and care of her. And that care had been extended to Harold, even if she had often felt it came from a sense of duty and not fatherly love and attention. But now, for whatever reason, he had changed. Perhaps Harold's misadventure had made William realize just how precious the boy was, how much he loved him after all.

But no, he had said such a frightening thing to her just before Bessie had interrupted them. Beth rubbed her head. It had been aching off and on ever since she had woke up, and now the pain was returning once more, making it hard to think.

The whole thing had her completely puzzled. William had always been someone she had thought cared overmuch about his fellowman. Surely it would be natural for that loving nature to have welcomed and loved his own child.

Suddenly she realized William had spoken to her again. She blinked and said rapidly, "I'm sorry, I was just remembering our first night ashore."

He stared at her a moment. "I was just telling you that the Pedlers had it even worse than we did," he said in a slightly husky voice. "A very cold wind blew, even though it was the twentieth of January. Apparently one of the women—Elizabeth, I think they said—slept in a large cask with three of her youngest children, but their eight-year-old boy had to stretch out on the spars on the side of a tent made of old sails."

He stopped abruptly. She thought she saw a flash of sadness in his eyes before he bent and put Harold down, saying gently, "Go and see if James is still asleep, little one, then stay with Lucy."

Harold's mouth drooped. Suddenly he put his hands on his hips, looked his father straight in the eye, and said belligerently, "No."

Beth stared at him in horror. She looked at William's stunned face and then quickly away, trying hard not to laugh. This was by no means the first time she had seen this type of rebellion from their usually angelic son and had had to deal with it, but she wondered curiously how William would handle this open defiance.

After a moment, when neither father nor son had said anything, she dared to glance at them.

William had put his hands on his hips and was staring steadily back at the rebellious, sturdy little figure in front of him. "I beg your pardon, Harold?" he said icily.

Harold glared back at him. Even more so did he look like his father. Her heart melted toward them both.

For another long moment the small figure hesitated. Then he dropped his eyes and his hands. One foot started to draw a small pattern in the dirt. "Want. . .wanta play wiv you, Farva," he said pleadingly.

Beth felt the smile stretch her face despite her efforts. William glanced at her swiftly before she could control her mirth. He looked pleased, helpless, and indignant all at the same time.

"I would like to play more, too, Harold," he said firmly after a moment, "but not now, especially with a little boy who just spoke to his father like that."

The brown eyes looked up at him and swelled with tears. Beth felt her own heart melt and was not in the least surprised when William kneeled down in the dirt and hugged Harold swiftly.

"But you won't do that again, will you, Harold?" he said gently. The little head shook in abashed agreement. Then his arms went up and hugged William back. "That's a good boy. We might be able to play later before bedtime, but now you must do what I said. Run in and stay with Lucy, please. I need to talk to Mother."

The little face only brightened a little, and Beth held her breath, half expecting further defiance. To her relief he gave in. She watched the small figure turn and trudge slowly to the house. When he had disappeared, she turned and peeped at William. He was studying her thoughtfully.

"Enjoyed that, did you, Mother?"

She stared at him uncertainly and then saw the twinkle in his eyes. Relieved, she smiled back. "No, I did not particularly enjoy seeing a son defy his father like that. But I did enjoy. . . Oh, William, he looked so much like you!"

All trace of amusement was wiped from his face in a flash.

Puzzled, she lost her own smile and said urgently, "What is it? Why do you look like that, William?"

He stared at her a moment longer and then closed his eyes. Alarmed, she stepped forward and put her hand on his arm.

"William?"

His eyes flew open. He put his hand over hers, the other went to her shoulder, holding her steady. "Beth, you really do believe Harold looks like me, don't you?" he bit out huskily, "I so want to believe he looks like me."

Utterly bewildered, she said slowly, "I have always believed it to be so."

Suddenly she knew his question had an importance to him that was beyond her understanding. Unless. . .

A little too quickly she added, "There is not a great physical likeness, although I have often noticed his smile is so much like yours. It lights. . .it lights up your whole face. Kind of starts in the depths of your brown eyes and then spreads all over your face. But his little mannerisms are becoming more and more like yours every day. I don't know how many times over the years I have seen you stand just so, your hands on your hips, your legs apart. . ." She faltered to a stop. His hands had tightened convulsively on her.

He was staring at her, searching her with such intensity that the fear which had not been far from her ever since he had acted so strangely yesterday began to increase alarmingly. The pain in her head started to throb. His fingers tightened even more and she winced.

Seemingly oblivious to her discomfort, he said urgently, "Beth, I know how weary you must be, but there is something we must talk about without further delay, and something I should tell you Robert Young said earlier." He swallowed and to her relief let go of her. Looking around he added, "Let's sit over there on that log. I don't want to risk Lucy hearing us."

She followed him and let him seat her with his usual, unconscious courtesy. Then he dropped onto the grass at her feet. Unable to say a word for the fear that now filled her, she waited.

"From what Robert said, I think John Martin is here looking for us."

She stared at him. Of all the things he wanted to talk about, this was the last thing she would have thought of.

"John is here, in South Australia?" she exclaimed with sudden delight. "But so soon after Kate's letter! Are you sure, William?" she asked eagerly.

Not looking at her, he pulled a long, narrow leaf off some grass near his feet and started to fold it over and over. Suddenly she realized his hands were shaking.

His obvious distress gave her courage. "William, please talk to me," she cried out. "What is it? Was it something. . .something in Kate's letter? I have been puzzled all day what you were so upset about before Bessie interrupted us. It's something to do with Harold, is it not?"

He raised his eyes and looked at her. The depth of sadness and misery in them frightened her even more. "I wish you had told me right at the beginning, Beth."

"Told you? Told you what?"

William stared at her. Utter bewilderment was her only expression. There was not the slightest sign of guilt.

He frowned suddenly. He thought he had learned every expression on her face over the years. Was there any chance her stepfather could have been mistaken after all? At first he had been so sure Lord Farnley was wrong, that somehow, whoever had told him had been nothing more than a malicious liar. But when he had found out it had been Percival, heir of Fleetwood. . .

Percival Farnley.

He drew in a sudden quick breath. Kate had said it had been Percival Farnley who had committed murder, had tried to kill them, who had lied. . .

For the first time in almost three years, hope burned in him again. "Beth, Beth, I have to know. . .is Harold my son?" he blurted out desperately and jumped to his feet.

She stared up at him blankly. He could see she was trying to comprehend his question. He knew when the implication of what he was asking suddenly hit her. Her eyes widened and every drop of color drained from her face.

She sprang to her feet. Her mouth opened and then closed as though she could not speak. Absolute horror filled her eyes.

"You. . .you. . .how dare you. . .dare you ask. . .such a dreadful thing!" she whispered at last.

William knew he had his answer. He also knew he had just made the most dreadful mistake any husband could make.

"You gave him the name John for his second name," he added in a daze, at long last bringing into the open what had perhaps convinced him the most, hurt him the most.

"John?" Her voice sounded as though it came from a great distance. "It was my own father's. . .my father's. . ."

"Beth. . ."

His choked, horrified whisper barely registered with Beth.

Trembling violently, she started shaking her head from side to side in violent negation that he could even think such a horrible thing of her. Fear was replaced by a sudden dreadful anger all mixed up with unbearable pain of heart and body.

Through a thick haze she saw William's hand go out to her. She raised her hand and struck out at it. She missed, but she whirled around and strode off, not caring where she went, just knowing she had to get away from him.

Then she felt his hands grasp her shoulders. He was trying to stop her, turning her around. Suddenly she was hitting out at him, slashing at his face, his chest, anywhere her fists could land until at last he managed to wrap his arms so tightly around her she could not move.

"Beth, stop it, Beth. Stop it! Oh, be still, my darling, you don't know what it's been like," he panted desperately. "These past years thinking, praying, hoping he was wrong. . ."

His words barely penetrated. Her head was aching so and suddenly every last ounce of energy drained from her. Her legs threatened to give way, and she leaned against him, hardly knowing she did so. Vaguely she knew he gave a tremendous groan. Then she felt his arms swing her up, clutching her to him.

For a moment he held her, then he gave a sharp exclamation and started swiftly toward the house. He stopped just as suddenly. A noise reached her then. Horses' hoofs, the rattle of harness, wheels crunching on the rough stones of the road.

She started to struggle again, and his grip tightened. She lashed out, this time catching him full across his face. His head twisted sideways, and he gave an angry "No! Behave yourself, Beth!"

Then a loud voice called out, " 'Ere, 'ere there, what's this, then? What you be doin' of with that lady, sir?"

Beth forced her eyes open. She looked straight up into William's contorted face. She stared at him, and when he looked down at her, she said in a harsh voice that sounded nothing like her own, "Put me down, please."

"Beth, I. . ."

"Better do like the lady says, mister," another voice interrupted sharply and with authority. "Put her down at once."

The last time she had heard those deep tones with the slight Spanish accent had been in another time. Another place. In a crowded, stifling courtroom.

She gave a startled exclamation. The arms holding her tightened and then slowly let her go, putting her on her feet, but still supporting her as she straightened.

"Oh," that voice spoke again. This time there was a trace of amusement. "Sorry, Reverend, er, Garrett, is it? Didn't see your clerical getup. Oh!"

The voice changed again as Beth raised her head and looked at him. She swallowed several times until she found her voice. Then she took a trembling step forward. William's hands dropped away.

"Hello, John," she said in a slightly hysterical voice. "You have perfect timing." She swung back a little wildly toward William. "William, I believe you never did meet the man you have obviously heard so much about."

Her head was throbbing very badly now, but she started to laugh and suddenly couldn't stop. The tears came then, even as she cried out wildly, almost incoherently, "Reverend William Garrett, I'd like to introduce you to my old friend. . .no, no, with what you believe, he could not just be that, could he? My dear husband, meet my old lover, John Martin!"

Then Beth, who had never fainted before in her life, for the second time in two days slipped into merciful oblivion.

seven

John Martin sprang forward to catch Beth, but William was before him, grabbing her as she started to sway and sweeping her up once more into his arms.

"Oh, God," he groaned out loud in a desperate prayer, "what have I done?"

"John, is that Beth and William?" an anxious woman's voice asked sharply.

William looked blindly up from Beth's still form toward the small carriage that had ground to a halt, its driver still trying to quiet the two horses. A woman was rapidly descending from it, and John Martin hastened to assist her.

"Yes, my dear, it is at last," William heard him say quickly, "but it seems we have appeared at an inopportune time."

He heard no more, too intent on carrying his precious burden to the house, yelling for Lucy to bring some water, putting Beth down on the couch in the front room, helplessly smoothing a few wayward strands of hair back from her pale forehead, patting her hands, calling in a tortured, panting voice, "Beth, I'm so sorry, so sorry, Beth. . ."

He was hardly aware that the two strangers had followed him until a gentle woman's voice said firmly, "Sir, she is stirring. Let me attend to her, please."

But he refused to move until two large, strong hands took him by the arms and firmly pushed him aside. "Best leave her to Elizabeth, Reverend Garrett. She is very good with sickness."

William stilled. He looked down at the hands still holding him. They were the hands of a man who had spent much time working in the merciless sun. They were deeply tanned. A twisted scar marred the surface of one. The faintest edge of other scars at the wrists disappeared beneath the well-cut sleeves of a dark coat.

Adam Stevens had similar scars. Scars from cruel manacles that had rubbed tender skin raw. Convict's scars. The hands let him go, and William shut his eyes tightly for a moment. It was so easy to preach about it, to exhort others to do it, but. . .

Jesus, Jesus, he prayed silently, desperately, *this is the man who has haunted me night and day for so many long months. Help me, help me.*

Slowly he raised his eyes. John was a big man, taller even than himself. He was as he had been described to him by Lord Farnley when he had asked if William had seen him at all around Fleetwood. Very Spanish in appearance, olive skin now tanned even darker, hair. . .hair that had been so much a part of the nightmare that had been William's every time he had looked at Harold's dark curls. But this man's hair was black, a definite black.

Realization stabbed at him that while Harold's head of curls was very dark, it was not like this, not like a raven's wing of gleaming, shining black.

His absorbed gaze lowered and encountered startling blue eyes.

"They should be brown eyes," he thought in a daze, and only realized he had spoken aloud when they suddenly brightened with astonishment, and then gleamed with some amusement.

John Martin said a little stiffly, "So I was repeatedly told while I was a child. Something of an aberration, I always thought, until I met my. . .my father, Lord Farnley."

Speechless, William stared at him. The man was right. His eyes were uncannily like his guardian's had been, a strong trait handed down from generation to generation of Farnleys.

Then Beth gave a slight moan and drew William's sole attention once again. The strange woman had swiftly loosened his wife's clothes, fanned her, and was now lifting her head to help her swallow a few mouthfuls of the water the hand-wringing Lucy had brought.

He suddenly became aware that something was tugging at his trousers. He glanced down and straight into Harold's frightened little face.

"Muvva fall down?" he whispered fearfully.

William dropped down to his level and drew him to his chest, hugging him tightly. This beautiful child he had failed miserably to keep from loving with all his heart in case it was ripped from him if John Martin claimed his son, this small child he loved so fiercely, was truly his son. His flesh-and-blood son!

"Did she fall over?"

William looked up blankly at the woman. What had John Martin called her? Elizabeth? "No, no," he choked out, trying to reassure her frowning face. "She. . .she had a bad shock, and on top of one yesterday. . ."

"Muvva?"

Harold wriggled, trying to push his father's arms away. William let him go and swung around as the small figure hurtled toward his mother and her outstretched hand.

Beth was watching them. The blankness in her eyes suddenly alarmed him even more than her outburst of anger had. Her arms closed around Harold, but it seemed to William she barely knew what she was doing as she softly murmured faint words to reassure the boy and then sent him off to Lucy.

"I think she should go to her room. She would be far more comfortable on a bed and probably just needs a good sleep," the woman's firm tones said.

William looked at the speaker. She was scowling at him. "Who are you?" he asked bluntly.

There was a slight movement behind him. "Beth certainly had a novel way of introducing the two of us." The laughter had disappeared completely from the man's blue eyes. They were watchful, studying William intently. Then they were directed at the woman, and a tender light filled them. He stretched out a hand. She put hers in it and raised her head proudly.

"May I present my wife, Lady Farnley?" John Martin said very formally. "Elizabeth, meet Reverend Garrett and his wife, Beth, who is Kate's, and now also my, stepsister."

A brilliant blush rose in his wife's face. She looked at John with considerable confusion, but there was no mistaking her pride and love for him. She looked back at William and suddenly swept him a curtsy that would have been acceptable in any fashionable drawing room. She murmured politely, "Reverend Garrett, Mrs. Garrett," and then spoiled all her dignity and gracious airs by allowing her eyes to dance and barely controlling a gurgle of laughter.

John Martin's face broke into a tender, indulgent smile. It transformed him, suddenly making him look much younger and giving some indication of how his experiences the last few years had prematurely aged him.

"You must forgive us, William; my new status in life was only confirmed by mail that arrived as we were leaving Sydney. Everything has happened so fast these last weeks, and we have really had little chance to become used to. . .to. . ." He paused, his face becoming solemn again. "To my new title."

He was married? His claims had been proven? He was in truth Lord Farnley's son and heir? And now also then, Beth's stepbrother, even as Kate was her stepsister while being John Martin's half sister?

William stared from one to the other, and then swung his astonished gaze to Beth. She was surveying Elizabeth and John with nothing more than mild curiosity. That blankness in her eyes suddenly frightened him immensely, "Kate did not say anything about you being married," he said sharply, still not looking away from Beth.

"Did she not?" There was impatience now in John's polite voice. "But I would still expect you to greet Elizabeth as my wife—and Lady Farnley," he added with a sudden snap in his voice.

With a tremendous effort, William pulled his gaze from Beth. He looked at John Martin a little vaguely. Those black eyebrows were lifted haughtily, and a stern look had replaced the twinkling eyes. Even so had another Lord Farnley looked at him after some youthful misdemeanor.

A sharp pang smote him. Like father, like son.

John's frown deepened at his continued lack of response. With great effort, William tried to pull himself together. Standing to attention, he gave a formal bow.

"I. . .we are very pleased to meet you, both. I trust your journey here was not too unpleasant? I only heard a couple hours ago. . ." He stopped. Was it really that short a time? His look darted back to Beth. Clearing his throat he said in a stilted voice, "I was only told after our church service this morning that someone was looking for us."

John suddenly relaxed and smiled amicably. "I've been making enquiries everywhere, hoping to find you while our ship is here. We did not think of you moving to the outer edges of the Adelaide district as you have."

Elizabeth said impatiently, "Yes, yes, I'm sure we have time for all this later. John, Mrs. Garrett—Beth—needs her bed. Right now." She too had followed William's gaze and was also watching Beth with a concerned frown.

William started forward, but stopped dead, rooted to the spot when Beth jumped and then shrank back and turned her head away.

"I. . .I. . .can manage," she whispered in a cracked voice.

He could not move as Elizabeth helped her sit up. Beth attempted to stand. She swayed and would have fallen. William instinctively took a step forward, his hand out, but she shrank away again and this time raised her head.

The blankness was gone. Her eyes were wild, filled with anguish as she panted, "No. No. . .don't touch me. Don't touch me. . .never again!"

For a moment no one moved, then Beth sank back onto the edge of the couch. She was shaking violently. Elizabeth raised shocked eyes to her husband. Some silent communication passed between them, and he moved swiftly forward and picked Beth up. Straightening, he asked grimly, "Where is her bedroom?"

Still William could not move. Lucy had returned moments before, and it was she who said in a trembling whisper, "This way, sir." They moved in procession from the room, Elizabeth hesitating for a brief moment before shrugging slightly and folowing swiftly after them.

Not until Harold ran to his side did William move. With a tremendous effort he tried to soothe the anxious little questions when his own were filling his heart and soul with something close to despair.

Desperately his heart reached out to the One who had alone been his source of strength and love for so long. "Help her, Father. Help her understand. Help her forgive me, even if she can never love me as I want her to."

❧

The touch of cool sheets barely registered to Beth. She looked up at John Martin as he laid her down. His face was a blur. She wiped the back of her hand across her eyes, and he came into focus. Still the same, handsome face she had known, but now more deeply lined, showing the ravages of the last few years.

"John. . . ," she said in a wondering, trembling little voice. "You. . .you're here. You're really here."

"Hello, Beth," he said gently. "Hush now. There will be time to talk later. You rest now. Elizabeth will look after you."

Then he was gone. He would be able to tell William. . .tell William the truth about their friendship.

But why bother now? Nothing mattered. William had been thinking such dreadful things about her. . .about Harold. Her feverish, confused mind was a jumble of thoughts. She was suddenly fiercely glad she had never quite plucked up the courage to expose her heart to him since her discovery during that wedding service, even though that love had continued to grow. It would be too, too humiliating if he knew how much she loved him.

He did not love her, could not love her. How could any man love her, thinking what he did?

William. . .especially the Reverend Garrett. . .could never love a woman he thought such a dreadful, immoral woman, a liar of the most shocking proportions, she thought hysterically.

Why, more than once in London she had heard him praying for some immoral woman, heard him preach to those poor, unfortunate women from the gutter, heard how he would try to persuade them to turn from their wicked ways, heard him quote a verse that for some reason had stuck in her mind.

What had it been? A proverb. She had it marked in her Bible.

"My Bible," she muttered and tried to sit up. "I want my Bible."

The pain in her head stabbed sharply. Vaguely she knew the strange woman was still in the bedroom. The back of a hand touched her forehead and the stranger. . .no, she wasn't a stranger. Had not John said something. . .? Ah, yes, his wife. It was his wife who was there with her, who was saying briskly, "As I thought, she has a fever."

"My Bible," Beth insisted.

"Yes, yes," the voice soothed. "I'll get it for you just as soon as you are more comfortable."

Beth subsided. She closed eyes that were burning now and was vaguely aware of the woman's firm voice saying, "Where are her night things?"

Lucy's trembling voice said, "Right. . .right here, ma'am."

Somewhere James was starting to cry. Like he did when it was time for her to feed him.

"James," Beth said faintly and tried to struggle up. Tha

awful pain jabbed her head again. Her head whirled, and then a soft, gentle voice was shushing her, telling her they would look after the baby. Lucy would go that moment. All she had to do was rest, sleep.

She looked up searchingly and with an effort focused on the stranger. The gentle but capable hands removing her clothes stilled. This was John Martin's wife—Elizabeth, he had called her. She was watching Beth with a peculiar expression on her beautiful face. They studied each other for a long moment.

Then suddenly, Beth's eyesight blurred once more. "I'm. . . I'm so. . .sorry. . .so sorry. . ."

A gentle finger touched her cheek, wiped away a solitary tear making its slow way down. "Hush now. Like John said, we can talk later, when you've recovered."

Obediently, she let hands do what they would with her. Docilely she swallowed something vile Elizabeth held to her lips. But she had been trying to remember. . .

"My Bible," she panted urgently.

"Yes, yes," the gentle voice soothed her. "It is here beside your bed, but later—"

"No, no! Must know the verse. . .must know. . . ," she whispered frantically.

There was a brief silence. Once more she strove to sit up.

"No, don't move," the voice said urgently. "I have your Bible. Which verse is it? I can read it for you, if you like."

Beth tried to think. Which verse? William quoted it. "Proverbs," she gasped, "there should be a book token there." Pages rustled. "I marked the verse. . ."

"This looks like it. Now, you have a mark beside Proverbs chapter 12 and verse 4," Elizabeth said softly. "It is about a virtuous woman. Is that the one?"

"Yes, yes. 'A virtuous woman is a crown to her husband: but. . .' I can't remember the rest," Beth whispered desperately, "I can't remember. . ."

There was silence. Then Elizabeth said softly, slowly, "It

says, 'but she that maketh ashamed is as rottenness in his bones.' Now, do relax, my dear," she added swiftly. "Whatever has happened, you are ill and must sleep."

Beth was still. Suddenly she muttered, "Maketh ashamed. . . rottenness. . .no, no!"

The pain in her head was mercifully easing at last. She had to think. . .think. . .

God's gift of sleep at last claimed her.

❧

William heard John Martin reenter the room and raised his head from its comforting place against Harold's soft curls. The child was sitting on his knees being distracted by his father's pocket watch, while the man had been staring into space, stricken, unable to move, unable to pray, hardly believing what Beth had said, how for the first time ever she had not wanted him near her.

"Is she all right?" he asked hoarsely.

"Elizabeth is seeing to her," the new Lord Farnley said shortly. "She says Beth has a fever."

"A fever!"

"Yes, but I think there is more than that, don't you?" There was a steely look in those bright, expressive eyes.

William stared at him and then shuddered and closed his eyes. They were silent a long moment, and then Lucy rushed into the room.

She paused, ringing her hands. "Sir, the lady, says to. . .to make some tea and to mind the children as I always do," she appealed to William in a frightened rush.

William put Harold down and with an effort said, "Yes, yes, you go about your tasks. Perhaps you could arrange some. . . some refreshments for our guests."

She bobbed, took Harold by the hand, and after another curious glance at the fashionably dressed stranger hurried away with the reluctant boy.

John said shortly, "I must speak to our coachman, and pay

his fee. It is satisfactory to bring our bags in?"

"Yes, yes, of course," William said in a choked voice. "I am sorry. You must of course stay the night. We. . .I. . .we will sort out a room for you," and then felt foolish as John merely nodded before disappearing.

William stared at the closed door. Then with a groan of anguish he sank down onto the nearest chair, buried his head in his hands, thinking of all that had happened, praying desperately. He had hurt Beth beyond belief. Gone was his hope of ever winning her love. Would she ever be able to forgive him?

Lord Farnley had been so devastated that day he had drawn William into his study the moment the young man had entered Fleetwood after an absence of too many months doing that very last frantically busy term at college. William's only desire had been to find Beth, to tell her how sorry he was her mother was so desperately ill, how sorry no one had told him so he could have at least written to her, telling her he was praying for them all as he always did.

At first he could not believe what his old guardian had been telling him, had in fact been furious! Beth, his sweet Beth, seen meeting a man many times in secret? His Beth seen kissing this man, a common farm workman? His Beth more than probably doing far worse with this worthless seducer? His Beth with. . .with child. . .ruined. . .

Impossible!

He had wanted to laugh in the older man's face, but then horror had filled him. There was no mistaking the man's depth of anguish, his dreadful disappointment in his stepdaughter, and his frantic desire to keep the scandal from his dying wife at all costs.

And then, he remembered that Lord Farnley had always shown special affection for the beautiful, fair daughter of his wife, even more, it had seemed at times, than for his own flesh-and-blood daughter, Kate. Whatever the old lord had been told about Beth, William had been forced to believe it was true.

At the time Lord Farnley had refused to tell William the name of the chief informer, merely assuring him vehemently it was not someone who would repeat idle, malicious gossip without proof, and had only done so in an attempt to preserve the good name of the family. It had only been later, after Harold's birth, that Lord Farnley had told William the informer had been his nephew, Percival Farnley.

Even though William had still not been able to really believe the worst of the information, he privately agreed that Beth might have been compromised by her actions, which he personally could see as nothing more than a sixteen-year-old's foolishness. So he had said nothing against Lord Farnley's earnest plea to marry her. After all, had not this been the burning wish of his heart since those last summer holidays at home when the girl who had been his old playmate and friend had suddenly been transformed into the most unbelievably sweet and beautiful woman he had ever seen?

He groaned out loud, and then started as a hand touched his shoulder briefly. "I just saw Elizabeth, and she says Beth has at last fallen asleep," John's voice said softly.

William rose and took a hasty step forward.

"She also said she thinks it would be best for you not to, ah, not to disturb them for awhile," John added hastily.

William stared at the other man and then said bitterly, "You mean, don't risk upsetting Beth again." His voice cracked and he turned away. Striding to the small window, he blindly stared out. It looked out on that part of the front yard where he had held the church service.

After a long silence he muttered, "I was foolish. It was too soon after yesterday's traumas."

"Yesterday's traumas?"

William barely heard the quiet words. He stood for another long moment, wishing he had suggested the following Sunday for the service. It had seemed fitting to want to give thanks immediately. But he had been selfish, keen to preach, to lead a service again, not thinking of his wife. It had been too much for her after the ordeal of the day before.

And then today he had blurted out his long-held fear in an unforgivable way. Perhaps if he had brought it all out into the open before, it might not have erupted like a volcano. For the last six months the evidence had been there before his eyes. There was no doubt James looked so much like Harold, and deep in his heart he had known the truth. Foolishly, he had still needed her to set his heart at rest after all the agonizing he had been through.

He should have trusted God more. He should have been more sensitive to His leading. He should have remembered that Beth had been slow to recover from James's birth. The long sea journey had deprived her of health and vigor. Living in those primitive conditions in that tent, even sleeping in that crowded bedroom throughout the cold winter had not been as restful as it should have been.

Then after the baby's arrival, he had been too busy to help her as he should. He had been trying desperately to get the house ready for them to move into as quickly as possible, and afterward, he had been busy clearing the ground, trying to start at least a small vegetable patch because fresh food was so hard to come by.

And of course, as soon as they had moved, Beth had gone into a whirl of activity to furnish the house, to make it a real home with what was available. The only help he had been able to get to come and live with them so far had been Lucy, an inexperienced young woman, kind and willing as she was. People prepared to be servants were few. Some had even grumbled that allowing convicts to live here might not be such a bad idea after all.

He had often thanked God for the Young family, but it was all still a far cry from the care Beth had received when Harold arrived in their comfortable apartment in London. Kate had been there to attend her, and plenty of servants. At the last moment, the nurse employed to go on the ship with them had fallen ill, leaving no time to find a replacement.

Now with James, there were two young children to care for, and despite all the help he had been able to give her himself, there was still far too much for Beth to do.

"What happened yesterday, William?" John asked softly again.

William turned around slowly. "Harold was lost in the bush. We had to search several hours for him," he said abruptly, reluctant to remember that terrible fear that they would not find the small boy by nightfall, perhaps not find him at all until it was too late.

John drew in a whistling breath through his teeth. "And Beth searched also? That's why she has those cuts on her legs," he murmured.

"On her legs? She said nothing about. . .I was unaware she had cuts there, only the small scratches on her face," he said sharply, and then immediately felt the natural reserve a husband should at this betrayal that he had not seen his wife's legs.

"Elizabeth told me they are quite nasty and red and no doubt have contributed to the fever."

Something like relief touched John's voice, and William stared at him blankly. Then his eyes narrowed, and he raised his chin and said indignantly, "I can assure you I have never laid a finger on her. In fact, it was Beth who found Harold."

"William," John said with horror in his voice. "I never thought for a moment you had caused them—perhaps someone else, but not you, especially when you intimated something had happened. Adam spoke so very highly of your faith and love of Christ. I could never believe you would hurt anyone, let alone your wife!"

William relaxed slightly. Belatedly remembering his manners, he gestured for John to be seated. He hesitated taking his own seat, still wanting to make sure that Beth was all right.

John noticed his glance toward the door and said sympathetically, "You would be best to leave her to Elizabeth." A slight, faraway look came to his face, and then he smiled slightly as William looked at him. "I can assure you from personal experience that she is an excellent nurse and will know just what is needed."

William remembered suddenly that one of the stories Adam had told them about John had been his severe illness on board ship and the care given to him by a woman, the daughter of a man he had worked for.

He cleared his throat. "We are so far. . .there are only two doctors in the colony. But I will fetch one if. . .if. . ." He faltered.

"Elizabeth will know whether we should send for one," John replied firmly, settling himself even further into the soft chair.

William looked at him. How did one behave, what did one say to this man he had heard so much about, the man he had thought he had much reason to hate? Beth's old lover.

eight

Whether John sensed William's discomfort or not, he made it easier for his host by asking, "Have you really decided to settle here in South Australia? And are you turning from the ministry to farming?"

William sat down opposite John and said with an effort, "We have almost decided to stay, but my continuing officially in the ministry will depend on the church authorities and my superiors. There is much need here," he finished simply, "for shepherds of God's flock as well as for farmers."

John looked around the small room and at the rough furnishings. "This is much more comfortable already than the home Elizabeth shared with me on Adam's property for many months," he murmured softly.

Curiosity stirred in William. "Adam told me how you and your convict friend showed the difference a personal devotion to Christ made in your lives so clear during those months you were working for him at Stevens' Downs that he too could not but come to believe in the Savior," he said impulsively.

John looked surprised and then embarrassed. He threw his hands out in a self-deprecating gesture. "The Holy Spirit had already been doing His work in Adam's life long before we met him. Elizabeth's mother was apparently a wonderful Christian woman."

"Your. . .your mother-in-law?"

"Yes, but she died several years ago, as did Elizabeth's father a while back. I deeply regret never meeting the Waverleys."

"The Waverleys? Your wife was a Waverley? I do remember they were the people who. . .who looked after Adam for several years."

John held his glance with a solemn look and then drawled, "You mean the master he was assigned to by those in charge of convicts, as I was, with my friend Timothy Hardy to Adam."

William stared at him. "I apologize," he said stiffly. "It was not my intention to remind you of something I am convinced you would much rather forget."

John looked thoughtful for a moment, then he said quietly, "There is much I do not like dwelling on, of course, yet I do rejoice in the knowledge that during all that happened to me, God never ceased to prove His love and faithfulness to me."

He cleared his throat and added steadily, "When Elizabeth convinced me I could marry her, even though I only had my ticket of leave then through the petitioning of a powerful friend of hers, our marriage was an act of faith in Him, in His promise to work all things out for good to them that love Him. We believed our love for each other was a precious gift from Him. It was a step of faith that I have never regretted." His voice choked, and he stopped abruptly. There was a wonderful light in his eyes.

William stared at him, remembering what Adam had privately confided to him about the harsh treatment convicts received and the cruel, unjust flogging in particular that John had endured so unjustly. He had also been challenged by the testimony Adam had given of the convicts learning to forgive, something he knew they would need to be ready to do again and again as the bad memories returned time after time.

"It has worked out for good," William repeated softly, and then in a stronger voice, he said sadly, "I have preached on that verse in Romans several times. By faith I believe it to be true, but now. . .now. . .when there is so much pain, it is so hard to hang on to that promise!"

John was silent, and then he said quietly, "If there is any way I can help you, I most certainly will." When William remained silent, he added hesitantly, "I do not want you to feel you must speak of what pains you, and it is obvious Beth was ill when she introduced us the way she did, but I. . .we. . ."

He paused, and still William did not, could not move.

"Beth was right the first time. We were never lovers, only ever friends except for one kiss."

William looked up sharply at that.

"Don't look at me like that, man," John said swiftly. "I swear to you it is the truth. How often when I was in that foul prison did I think of those beautiful, stolen hours spent with a very young, innocent girl not long out of the schoolroom. I was lonely, very lonely, wondering what to do, how to present myself to Lord Farnley as the son he had long thought had died with my mother, fearing he would not acknowledge me. Beth was very beautiful but also so desperately unhappy, confused, missing you."

William's eyes widened.

"Oh, yes." John smiled tightly. "It seemed as though you came into every conversation. It was 'William said this' or 'William said that.' And I started to feel quite jealous of your place in her affections. That very last day we met before. . . before I found old Jock Macallister murdered, she was talking on and on about you coming home the very next day. It annoyed me immensely. She was in a very happy mood, the happiest I had ever seen her, despite her worry over her mother's illness."

He swallowed, but continued steadily. "I had become very fond of her, even thought perhaps we might start to love each other. I am still somewhat ashamed of taking advantage of her, she was so young, although afterward. . ." He paused and hurried on. "I lost my head and kissed her, kissed her quite passionately that day, I'm afraid. So much so, it frightened the life out of her, and she ran straight off home."

William suddenly felt quite ferocious. This man had kissed Beth, his Beth!

"Oh, there is really no need to look at me like that, man," John said with more than a trace of impatience. "We were never lovers! I never even saw her after that until today. I was arrested within the hour and hauled off to prison."

Lucy knocked on the door, and William was relieved to be able to turn his attention to offering his guest refreshments. After they were alone again, William said in a stilted voice, "I do thank you for confiding what you have, but I would be pleased if we talked of something else now."

"Of course, of course," John said swiftly. "Perhaps you would not mind telling me something about the adventure your son had yesterday."

Rather to his surprise, William found himself telling John quite comfortably about the events of the last couple days, even about the aboriginal's part in finding Harold. John was very interested in all that he said, asking questions about the Youngs, and then especially about the aboriginals in the area. On that subject, William had to admit to an appalling lack of knowledge.

"I feel very sorry for the aboriginals," John said gravely. "As well as being dispossessed of their lands, their numbers have been sadly depleted by our diseases which they have no resistance to."

William frowned. "Someone yesterday mentioned that their numbers are not great in the Adelaide plains, only a few hundred as far as anyone knows. The scars of smallpox are apparently on many of them. From what has been ascertained and from what they claim, the disease spread here from contact with the eastern tribes, and a great many died some years ago before the first settlers arrived. They are retreating to the fringes of the settlement."

"And as more emigrants arrive, those fringes ever move farther out."

Both men were silent, and then John said proudly, "Elizabeth has long had a real burden for the plight of the aboriginals in her property's area. In fact, she is absolutely thrilled that Kate and Adam are more than happy to continue her work among them at Waverley."

"Work among them?" William said thoughtfully. "Would you tell me what she has been doing?"

Enthusiastically, John started explaining the details of the health and education programs that Elizabeth had begun, as well as the attempts to teach them about Jesus Christ. But he had barely started when Elizabeth came into the room hastily, her face grave.

William sprang to his feet. "Beth. . . ?"

"She slept for only a brief time, and now she is very restless," Elizabeth said quickly. "I have only the barest amount of medicines with me, and I think perhaps a doctor should be sent for."

William stood stunned, and John said quickly, "It is as you thought then. William, I took the liberty of asking the man who brought us here to find a doctor on his return and ask him to attend us."

Without a word, William rushed from the room. Beth was lying very still when he sank down beside her bed, but several moments later she begun muttering and tossing to and fro in the bed as though having a nightmare.

"Harold!" she suddenly called out clearly, "Harold, where are you?" Her voice faded again into unintelligible groans.

William took her restless hands, holding them to his face. "Harold is safe, Beth. He is safe in his bed."

Her restless movements stilled, and she relaxed. Suddenly her eyes flew open and she called out, "William, William?"

"I'm here, Beth. . ." His voice choked, but then he said steadily, "I'll always be here, Beth."

Her thin hands suddenly clenched his, but then she relaxed and was still again.

How long William sat beside her he did not know. While Elizabeth and Lucy cared for her other needs, constantly sponging her hot body, changing the hot sheets, in a desperate attempt to lower her temperature, it was only his hands that calmed her feverish restlessness, his voice that soothed her feverish fears.

That fact eased the ache in his heart just a little. The light faded from the room, candles were lit, and then there was the welcome bustle at last of the doctor's arrival. When William eagerly looked up he was very pleased to see it was Dr. Thomas Cotter, the officially appointed colonial surgeon who had arrived in the settlement at its very beginning.

He looked with some awe toward John, who smiled briefly and murmured, "I told the coachman to make sure he brought only the very best doctor in Adelaide." And no doubt paid him accordingly, William realized, and he managed to smile his thanks back.

Even though the doctor was such an important person, William politely but adamantly refused to leave the room while he examined Beth. He had already seen the red, angry cuts that Elizabeth had bathed, treated with foments to try and draw the poison, and he had felt the pain of them as his own. He should have been more discerning, more aware that the mother would care for her babies first, not worry about cleansing her own wounds properly.

After a series of sharp questions, Dr. Cotter gave his patient a thorough examination. After considering the inflamed cuts, he held a strange, narrow, cylindrical instrument to Beth's chest, listening carefully with his ear at the other end.

William looked at him with some surprise. He had heard of this way of listening to the internal chest and abdominal sounds and was glad this doctor in a colony so far from England at least had such modern equipment.

When at last the doctor had finished, he stood back with a frown on his face, watching his patient. She called out again for Harold and William as she had so many countless times the last hour, and again William hastened to soothe her.

When she was quiet again, he looked helplessly up at the doctor, filled with guilt and anguish.

Dr. Cotter smiled slightly at him and said reassuringly, "She certainly has a bad infection, but she has been given just the right care immediately. If we can keep this fever down, she should do quite well." He looked with approval at Elizabeth's concerned face. "Her lungs seem quite clear, but tell me. . ." He paused and then asked gravely, "Has she had a bad shock of some kind?"

There was silence. The doctor looked from one to the other, and then at William.

"Shock? Unfortunately she has had several in the last two days," William said briefly.

He knew what the doctor was saying and closed his eyes briefly. His reaction to Kate's letter had undoubtedly shocked her. The whole episode with Harold had badly shocked her as well as exhausted her. Then he had so stupidly blurted out his question when she must already have had the poison from her infected legs burning up her body. Even John and Elizabeth's arrival had been a shock. It had all been too much for Beth, and was as much the cause of her fever as the infection.

"Right," the doctor was saying briskly to Elizabeth. "Normally I would advocate putting her whole body in a cool bath to bring down her fever, but it may be too much for her, another shock to her already overstretched mind and body. Keep bath-ing her as you have been doing. I have salves for her legs, medicine to help the fever, but above all. . ."

His last words were directed toward William, his voice and face stern. "She must be protected from anything that will disturb her mind. No more upsets; even the slightest may hinder her complete recovery."

No one moved. Then William looked down at Beth's deathly pale features and vowed, "I will see to that, you can be assured, Doctor. No more upsets."

He was grimly determined it would be so, but was not even sure how that could be prevented, especially when Beth once again knew what was happening around her.

It was dark when Beth woke. Only the faint light of a single candle flickered in the room. Vaguely she wondered why she had not blown it out before getting into bed. Then she remembered. William had asked her that dreadful question.

Before she could move, she was aware that somewhere close by in the room a low voice was murmuring very softly. William's voice.

She froze. How dare he be in her bedroom after what he had asked her, after what he had thought about Harold! She started to sit up, but just then his voice rose, and she stilled. He was speaking to someone. She strained to listen. Why. . .why, he was praying! She strained to hear.

"O Lord Jesus, please let me know Your will about this. Make it plain. Am I wrong in believing You have work for me to do for You here? Show me clearly, I pray. And for Beth. . ."

She started on hearing her own name. "William," she said loudly.

To her surprise her mouth was very dry, her voice hardly more than a cracked whisper. She swallowed, moistened her lips, and tried again in a louder voice.

"William, please go and do your praying in your own room."

There was utter stillness, and then he appeared beside her. His form was shadowy, and she could not see his face clearly.

"You're awake!"

"Of course, I'm awake," she said crossly. "Who could help waking up with you praying out loud like that?"

His hand reached out and touched her forehead. She lifted her hand to push it away and was astonished that her arm felt so heavy. Then his strong fingers caught hers, and he spoke in such a choked voice she wondered if he were sick.

"I've been doing a lot of praying in here the last couple of days, and this is the first time it has disturbed you."

She frowned. Vague images of people prodding and poking her, forcing her to drink horrible-tasting things came to her mind. "I've been ill," she said faintly.

His hand tightened on hers. "Yes, Beth, my darling," he said quietly, "you have been very ill, but your fever has eased now."

He let her go, and suddenly she wanted to cling to him, but he was moving toward the door. "I promised Elizabeth faithfully that I would let her know the moment you were awake," he said, and then he disappeared.

Elizabeth? She thought carefully. There had been a woman in that dreamworld that must have not been dreams after all, but fever, sickness.

Then there was a rustle of silk and soft, rapid footsteps. Beth blinked in the sudden extra light and stared up at the woman's face.

"Oh," she said in that scratchy, harsh voice which seemed all she could manage, "you are John's wife."

There was a soft, pleased laugh. "Yes, that is perfectly right, and I am very pleased you are so much better at last."

Beth started to feel agitated. There was something she had to ask John to tell William.

"William," she panted and tried to sit up.

Pain stabbed her in the leg, and only then did she realize it was heavily bandaged.

"William!" she cried out in a panic.

"I'm here, Beth," his quiet voice said.

Sudden fear welled up in her. Irrational fear, but she did not want to talk to him.

"No, no, go away, go away," she cried out.

Then she realized she was crying, great wrenching sobs. Elizabeth was there, soothing her, coaxing her to drink more of her horrible drinks. But William had gone, and she felt empty, alone as she never had before, until once more the sedative took over and she slept.

nine

Beth felt so tired. She found it hard to be interested in what was going on around her. At regular intervals she obediently swallowed the tasty broths and then the more solid foods Elizabeth permitted her. And in between she slept and slept.

She fed James as regularly as she could, although because of the state of her health she was being forced to wean him far too early. This should have worried her more than it did, but thinking about it just seemed too much effort. Harold was brought to her for only brief periods when she asked to see him, but once assured both children were well, she was only too happy for them to leave so Mother could have her sleep.

She was astonished how much strength she had lost after only a couple days in bed.

When she mentioned this to Elizabeth, she looked thoughtful for a moment and then said quietly, "Beth, dear, I think your tiredness is far more than the result of an infected leg. The sea voyage must have been very trying for you. From what I can understand, you have been working extremely hard since you arrived here, and I doubt if you even allowed your body sufficient rest after James was born. You have exhausted yourself, and now your body is letting you know it."

She hesitated as though she would like to say more, but smiled instead and added softly, "Just rest and sleep as much as you want for the moment."

Beth was forced to silently agree with this woman who had so quickly become such a good friend. Physically she was exhausted, but she realized this was more a weariness of her soul and spirit.

The fever had disappeared altogether after those first

dreadful, dream-filled nights and days. The doctor permitted her to stand as soon as the fever had abated and the red streaks up her legs had disappeared. Humbly she had accepted the doctor's mild scold at permitting them to become so infected without seeking attention.

That first day out of bed her legs trembled violently, but as the days passed and she was gradually allowed to be up in a chair for longer periods, she still refused to leave her room. She could not explain the feeling of panic that came every time she thought of doing so.

John visited her very briefly each day when Elizabeth was with her, but Beth did not know what to say to him. There was so much that should be said, perhaps needed to be said, but when she had tried, hesitantly mentioning Fleetwood, he had immediately put her off, patting her hand and saying there was no need to talk about all that just yet. With considerable relief, she had subsided.

Not once did William enter the bedroom, and not once did she mention his name. Many times she heard his voice in the house, his even tread pause outside her room. She would close her eyes, hold her breath, hoping he would enter, afraid he might. Her confusion about him distressed her greatly. She wanted to see him quite desperately one moment and hated him fiercely the next.

And so the days drifted by. For the most part, she simply sat and stared through the window of her bedroom at the leaves of the tall gum tree that gave the house shade. Although spring had officially arrived, it had turned very cold, and the fire in the bedroom was kept burning. Beth often shivered, but not always from the wintry chill.

Day after day Beth just could not be bothered getting out of her nightclothes. Elizabeth eventually insisted she dress each day. One morning after Beth had reluctantly dressed herself, not really caring how she looked, she finished forcing down a few mouthfuls of a late breakfast just as Elizabeth breezed into her bedroom after a brief knock.

She greeted Beth cheerfully and then said, "Good, you are already up and finished your breakfast. You have some visitors."

Beth stared at her. "Some visitors? I really don't think. . ."

"And they have called many times inquiring most anxiously after you," Elizabeth said brightly as though Beth had not spoken. "I am afraid today I just have not had the heart to say no to them once again. A Mrs. Young and her daughter Bessie have walked quite some distance in the freezing wind to visit you. And William and John have gone into town today. Now, you have not yet brushed your hair? That will never do, or your friends will think you are sadly neglected."

William was not at home. She would not risk meeting him.

Beth tried a feeble protest, but almost before she knew it, she had been fussed over, tidied, and was being escorted from the room.

She was still not at all strong, but was astonished at the gasp of horror Mrs. Young gave as soon as she saw her leaning on Elizabeth's arm and blurted out, "Oh, my dear, how thin you have become in such a brief time!"

Elizabeth gave a short, significant cough as she led Beth to a chair.

The good woman recovered herself immediately, saying with a beaming smile as she hastened forward to kiss Beth's cheek, "But it is so good to see you are on the mend, and you will soon have some color back in those pretty cheeks for sure. We have all been so concerned for you, and so pleased your stepbrother and his wife arrived at the right time to help care for you."

Her stepbrother. Of course, John was her stepbrother.

Beth looked across at Elizabeth suddenly and saw she was watching her with an anxious expression deep in her eyes. Suddenly she realized how much she had taken for granted all that this woman had done for her since she had collapsed.

She smiled mistily at Elizabeth and said earnestly, "No one could be more fortunate in her sister, Isabel."

Elizabeth stared and then beamed happily back at her. "And I have been an only child and am so very pleased to have a sister since I married John. In fact, two sisters," she said with a delighted laugh.

Bessie shyly greeted Beth, and said fervently, "I am so glad you are better, Mrs. Garrett."

Beth looked at the young girl dressed in her very best dress and smiled gently at her. "Elizabeth tells me you have been a great help with both the boys, Bessie, dear."

Big tears filled the girl's eyes. "I've felt so bad about Harold," she whispered.

Beth sat up a little straighter. "Oh, Bessie, surely you are not still blaming yourself for his escapade, are you?" she exclaimed.

"There, didn't I keep telling you Mrs. Garrett was not angry with you," Mrs. Young said with satisfaction. "The foolish child has been fretting herself silly."

For the first time, Beth noticed the black circles beneath the girl's eyes and her drawn face. "Oh, Bessie, my dear, dear girl," she said earnestly, "not for a moment did either his father or I blame you. We know how quick he can be, how naughty at times. It is very good of you even to mind him for us as well as you have."

Relief swept across the girl's face, but the tears started in earnest. Beth stood and moved swiftly toward her. Crouching down beside the girl's chair, she put her arms out and hugged the thin young body, letting her sob on her shoulder a few moments before saying in a bracing tone, "Now do stop crying, or whatever will Harold think if he finds his friend like this?" She thought of something and added slowly, "He will think you have fallen down and hurt yourself, as he did when I first became sick."

She stood up and looked quickly at Elizabeth. She was

watching her with a worried frown, and suddenly she realized how much she had sheltered her from thinking in any detail about that horrible day.

"I think we could all do with some tea, don't you, Elizabeth?" she said softly with a gentle smile and then quickly sat down again because her legs had started to tremble.

Elizabeth was still and then slowly smiled back a little tremulously. Her eyes gleamed suspiciously, but she said brightly, "I took the liberty beforehand of asking Lucy to bring us some. Ha, I think this must be her now."

She whirled from her chair to hold the door wide for a flushed Lucy, who almost tripped in her eagerness to enter the room with her heavily laden tray. She beamed at Beth excitedly, and again Beth realized how much these good people cared for her.

They were also very thoughtful, chatting lightly about local gossip and not lingering over their refreshments. Mrs. Young rose and said their good-byes firmly. "We must not tire you too much on our first visit," she added briskly before kissing Beth's cheek, bidding Bessie make her curtsy, and taking her daughter swiftly away.

Beth looked after them and then slowly turned to Elizabeth. "Thank you," she said simply.

Elizabeth flushed slightly, but did not pretend she did not know what she was being thanked for. "You have been in danger of slipping into a serious decline," she said gently, "and we have been at our wit's end to know the best thing to do," she added bluntly. "Especially when you have not even shown much interest in your children or. . ." She hesitated and then added resolutely, "Or your husband."

Beth stared at her. Bitterness stabbed her, and ignoring the reference to Harold and James, she said fiercely, "And I do not see that he has shown very much interest in his wife!"

Shock registered on Elizabeth's face, and she cried out, "Oh, how could you say so? William never left your side the whole time you were delirious. He was the only one who could soothe you. We could not even persuade him to lie down on his bed for a couple hours sleep. He insisted on a mattress beside your bed. It was only <u>after</u> you woke properly and cried out at him to go away that he has not dared to approach you, except I suspect he has crept into your room when you have been sound asleep to assure himself you were improving, and all because—" She stopped abruptly, her hand going to her mouth.

Warmth was swelling, growing inside Beth, dispelling the chill that seemed to have been her constant companion ever since she had woke from her first natural sleep and William had not been there.

"I told him to go away?" she gasped in horror. "Surely not," she wailed suddenly. "I so wanted his arms around me, but when he did not come I thought he had such a disgust of me that. . .that. . ."

Elizabeth stared at her, and then exclaimed, "Of course. How stupid we are. I should have known you were still not in your right senses."

Beth stared at her in horror. She opened her mouth and snapped it shut at the sound of horses outside. Both women stiffened.

"I. . .I must go to my room," Beth stammered in sudden fright.

"I think it is too late for that," murmured Elizabeth, just a little triumphantly. She jumped to her feet and darted toward the door as heavy footsteps approached. John's laughing voice rang out. Elizabeth said something inaudible to Beth.

Beth tried to stand, but she heard William's voice say heartily, "Tea in the drawing room? Very good. That road was very dusty." Her legs were suddenly trembling so much she sank down weakly again just as William strode into the room.

He stopped dead. "Beth," he cried in a glad voice, "my dear, you are up!"

He took a few more eager strides toward her and then

stopped once more. She nearly cried out as the happy, welcoming smile disappeared abruptly and his face lost its color. He drew himself up and gave her a slight bow. "I must apologize, madam, I was unaware you were in here," he said in an expressionless voice and immediately turned to leave.

"William!" she cried out breathlessly.

He spun around, an anxious look on his face. "You are well. Do you need something?" he asked sharply.

She stared at him. If her appearance had shocked Mrs. Young, his drawn, thin face and deeply sunken eyes equally shocked her. "You. . .William, you look dreadful!" she whispered.

A cold look wiped out his obvious concern for her. "Then I will relieve you of having to endure my appearance," he bit out and once more started to leave the room.

"Please," she called out frantically. "Have you been ill also? Are you quite well? Is that why you have not been to see me?"

He stopped once more and stood very still, watching her carefully. "I have not been to see you because you became so distressed and then. . .then you told me to go away."

Her eyes widened. "No, no," she whispered, "I could never tell you that."

The sudden hope that flashed into his eyes brought tears close to her eyes. "You also told me earlier that day you could not bear me to touch you."

There was such pain in his voice that the tears spilled over, and immediately he was crouching beside her chair. "No, no, Beth you must not upset yourself. The doctor expressly forbade it," he murmured urgently.

"And you think that not seeing you all these long dreary days has not upset me?" she protested angrily.

He looked taken aback and said swiftly, "He said you were already under too much stress and must have no further upsets or he would not be responsible for the consequences. I thought. . .you said. . ."

Furiously she swiped at the tears rolling down her cheeks,

and to William's obvious astonishment actually snorted. "And obviously he has only been attending gently nurtured society ladies, not a pioneer minister's wife and mother!"

That earned her an abrupt laugh, and she felt a large handkerchief being thrust into her hands. "But Beth," he said softly, "until you married me you were a gently nurtured society girl."

She used the handkerchief effectively and straightened. For a moment she glared at him and then slowly subsided. She looked down at the handkerchief and started twisting it.

"I've changed, William," she whispered in a choked voice. There was no answer and she looked up swiftly, surprising a sadness on his face that smote her deeply.

His lips moved in that lopsided smile that had always made her want to do whatever was necessary to make him smile properly. "Not too much from my dearest friend of so many years, I trust," he murmured.

Was she still his dearest friend then? Even though he had thought such horrible things about her?

Beth nearly blurted out the questions, but a sudden fear that he would only be prevaricating if he said of course she was his dearest friend stopped her from speaking. She knew that she would never be able to go along with such a lie. A deep pang clutched her. But she would settle for friendship, if that was all he could offer.

After a long moment, she took a deep breath and put her head on one side. "Well, I hope I've changed enough that if the Youngs had an orchard like the one at the Macallisters' place I'd not want to climb a tree and pelt you with rotten peaches anymore," she said in a serious voice.

Then she grinned suddenly and was very gratified that the sadness from his dark eyes disappeared. The dark chocolate-rich eyes lit instead with that glorious smile that seemed merely a reflection of a greater light that was always within him.

Then they were both chuckling at the memory of their youthful escapade that had brought the full wrath of Jock

Macallister upon them both and a complaint to Lord Farnley about his ward and his new daughter. If tears were not far behind her laughter, that would remain her secret alone.

"Trouble was, not all of those peaches were rotten, Mrs. Garrett, ma'am!"

"And Mr. Macallister had just arrived to pick the last of the crop for his good wife to make her preserves!" Beth chuckled again, and then her smile faded. "He was a good man, Jock Macallister."

"Aye, that he was," said a deep, somber voice from the doorway.

William stood up hastily, looking a little confused at being discovered with his arms around his wife's waist.

"Hello, John," Beth said a little shyly. She watched John advance into the room with his wife on his arm.

He smiled slightly at them both, but there was a shadow on his face, and she wished fervently he had not been reminded of old Jock's tragic death and its consequences. But before she could say so, he said quickly, "I'm very sorry to interrupt you both, but has William told you yet that unfortunately today is our last full day with you?"

"Oh, no," Beth cried out. "Elizabeth, you never said."

"I did not know," she said with a scowl. "John and William left early this morning to do business in town and ensure our ship was still scheduled to leave when we had been told, only to discover the captain wishes to leave earlier than originally planned. I thought we had at least another two days here."

Beth looked at them both and then helplessly back at William. "We. . .we have not talked about any. . .any of the past yet."

He smiled gently at her. "John and I have spoken a little about what happened."

Frustration surged through her and she cried out, "But I have not! And every time I have mentioned Fleetwood, John and Elizabeth both have refused to talk about it!"

William looked suddenly worried. "Beth, you must not distress yourself so. Dr. Cotter especially said you must not be allowed to get upset."

She gritted her teeth. "And you think that not talking about the past does not upset me? That knowing these last three years and more that my self-absorption, my self-pitying, my cowardice meant a good friend was in dire need and I did nothing, did not even know, has not upset me? And when I did eventually find out he had been accused of something dreadful, something I knew he could not possibly have done, that I did nothing has not upset me?"

She turned to John. He had gone a little pale and was very still. Passionately she cried out, "It has lain on my heart like a heavy stone. You told me I was the only real friend you had in all of England. I believed you, and yet I failed you miserably. You had even kissed me, and I never sent you a word of sympathy, of friendship! And then I found out you are my own stepbrother! And I am so ashamed, so ashamed! Do you think that has not upset me?"

William sucked in a quick breath, and John stood as though he had been turned to stone.

It was Elizabeth who rushed forward and threw her arms around Beth's tense figure. "There, there, I am sure you had many reasons why you did not contact John. Have I not been telling you ever since we got here, John, that Beth is not the kind of person to have turned her back on you the way you thought she had?"

John still did not move. Beth was dry-eyed, her face flushed as she stared at him above Elizabeth's head.

Then she dared to look at William.

He seemed dazed. "Is that why you insisted on coming with Kate and Adam all the way to Australia to find John, Beth?" he asked urgently.

She felt bewildered for a moment. She looked from him back to John and knew suddenly what he had thought. At the very least she would want Harold to meet his natural father!

Anger stirred in her and she said shortly, "Well, it most certainly was not for the reason it seems you may have thought!"

He looked stricken.

She suddenly could not bear his pain and looked again at Elizabeth. Beth thought back to that day at Fleetwood over twelve months before. Adam Stevens and Kate had just found John's lost papers that proved a son had been born to Lord Farnley's Spanish bride in Spain and that he had not died with his mother as the grief-stricken soldier had been told by her revengeful relatives.

"I am not sure what was the main reason. I knew I had to accompany Kate," she said slowly. "Guilt at my neglect of John was certainly one of the reasons, but there were others. I shared Kate's need to do what Father had wanted to do just before he died, to find his son and let him claim his rightful inheritance. It was the very last thing we could do for him and Fleetwood. We both knew it would have been so quickly brought to rack and ruin by Percy's mismanagement.

"To at least right that wrong for John seemed to be another essential reason, but then, at the forefront of my mind was that we perhaps could do something to change John's conviction, or at the very least ensure his life as a convict was endurable."

John gave a sharp exclamation, and she added swiftly, "Of course, then the lawyers said if your claim to be a peer of the realm was proven you could then ask for a retrial by your peers at the House of Lords."

"And that has not been necessary, because of Percival Farnley's confession," Elizabeth said swiftly.

"Yes, thank God," Beth said thankfully.

She looked at John, but he was looking at Elizabeth. She shook her head at him slightly, and Beth wondered what the silent messages passing between them meant.

Beth gave a wry smile and added hurriedly, "Another reason was Kate. I knew from that very first day how attracted she was to Adam Stevens. We knew nothing of him, and I was not absolutely sure we could trust him as much as she said we could. To my way of thinking she needed a chaperone, or at least someone close to her if things went wrong out here. Of course, when I realized I was pregnant, I. . .I nearly did not go."

She stopped, bit her lip hard to stop its sudden quiver, took a deep breath, and said slowly, "But the main reason was you, William. You seemed so eager yourself to come to this new country."

William simply stared at her and without taking his eyes off her sank down onto the nearest chair.

"I. . .we. . .don't you remember we praycd about this together, William?" One of the rare times they ever had. She pushed the thought away and added swiftly, "It was only afterward that I started feeling ill in the mornings and suspected I was having another baby. You had said you believed it was what God wanted us to do," she finished simply. "So after that, I knew even being pregnant would not stop us coming here."

"You. . .you came because in the end it was what you thought I wanted to do?"

She looked swiftly away from the dawning look of wonder on his face. Shyly she said, "When you believe something is God's will, nothing stops you from doing it, William. I knew we had to go."

No one spoke. At last John moved for the first time since her initial outburst. He came right up to Beth and crouched down until he was at her eye level.

"Beth," he asked quietly, "why did you not at least agree to testify that I was with you that morning Jock was killed?"

Her eyes widened. "Testify? Agree to testify? Whatever do you mean?"

Elizabeth said sharply, "John, is this really necessary, especially now?"

It was William who answered. "Yes, Elizabeth, I believe it

is," he said wearily. "As Beth said, we have not talked about the events in England yet, and you are leaving tomorrow. If there is anything at all that John needs to know it should be asked now. I. . .we. . .Beth and I have proved that it is important to ask questions and not think we know the answers."

John frowned, looking from him to Beth curiously. He hesitated as if to ask what he meant, and Beth was relieved when instead he said, "William has told us that Kate told you in her letter about Percival Farnley's part in my misfortune, but now I am wondering if we have yet to realize the extent of his mischief." He hesitated, swallowed, and looked again at Elizabeth.

She came to his rescue, saying swiftly, "When I first met John on board ship, I found out that besides being devastated about his wrongful conviction for Jock's death, he was very bitter. He believed you had completely ignored his letters and his urgent messages to come forward and swear in court that you had been with him in the upper meadow and that he could not possibly have been in the woods when Jock was killed."

Beth gasped and her hand went out to John. "But I received no word from you! Not a word! And when I found out you had been imprisoned for weeks, that made me very sad. Besides," she frowned thoughtfully, and then looked pleadingly across at William, "were we not told Jock was killed the very day you came home from college?"

He nodded silent agreement, and she cried out, "Don't you see, John? That was the day after we. . .our last meeting."

They stared at each other. "Oh, John," she said with a sob, "I swear I never received any word from you of any kind, and whoever told you they had given me any lied horribly."

"Percy." William's tone was flat, expressionless. "It was he who informed your father that the murderer of his gamekeeper had been apprehended. He also told him in my presence that he need not concern himself about the matter any further, that as your mother was so ill he would act as his uncle's deputy."

Wordlessly, John looked at William and then back at Beth. He looked stunned.

"Oh, John, John, don't you see?" Beth pleaded. Tears started rolling down her cheeks in a torrent. "Percival was just making sure you would be convicted. Please, please believe I did not even know you had been arrested until the very day before your sentencing by that horrible judge! I only just made it to that dreadful courtroom a little while before he. . .he. . .I thought he was going to hang you!" She was shaking badly by the time she finished speaking.

William strode forward. "That's enough. No more now. This is too soon."

He swept Beth up into his arms, and it was heaven to hear his strong voice protecting her, feel his familiar arms around her, holding her safely as he strode toward her bedroom.

Instinctively she clung to him, turning her head into his shoulder and letting the tears wash away the memory of that day so soon after her mother's funeral when she had managed to elude William and make her way to where the trial was being held.

"Oh, William, William, it was dreadful," she sobbed.

"Hush now," he whispered, "hush now," and went to put her on her bed. But she clung to him even tighter, so he sat on the bed, cradling her body in his arms, rocking her silently until her storm of tears had abated.

When she was still, he continued to silently hold her until at last she stirred, opened her eyes, and looked up into his face and asked huskily, "Do you remember that afternoon I arrived back at Fleetwood so ill a few weeks after we were married?"

Their eyes locked. William answered in a steady voice, "That evening I called the doctor so urgently, and he told me you were suffering from nothing more than many women suffer in the early months of expecting a baby."

She nodded. "I had just returned from the trial."

His arms tightened convulsively around her.

She continued in a rush, relieved that at last she could talk to him about those dark days that had haunted her for so long. "The evening before Mother had died. I had needed to get away from. . .from the house. I wandered down to the stables. Tom, our old groom, told me about the trial. I was shocked beyond measure, horrified. Not for a moment could I believe the young man I thought I had gotten to know so well and who had spoken so affectionately of Jock Macallister could have killed him.

"Tom was very upset and worried. He had known John and I had been friendly, and he was still trying to come to grips with the fact that he had not done anything to stop me from associating with a murderer. But as we talked, he at last expressed his doubts about John's guilt. In the end I persuaded him to drive me to the trial.

"But we were too late. John had already been declared guilty. I had gone there. . .oh, I'm not sure now just why I went, what I thought I might be able to do at such a late stage," she said wearily, "but I had started feeling so ill by the time we got there. I thought it was only travel sickness, but the heat. . .that horrible crowd wanting blood! As the minutes passed, I became worse. In fact, I was violently sick just outside the courthouse."

"I know."

She jerked upright. "You. . .you knew! But Tom promised me faithfully—"

"It wasn't Tom," he interrupted. "It was your dear cousin making more mischief. He took great delight in telling me he had seen you there, and that was just one more reason why. . ."

He stopped and pushed her onto the bed, saying a little desperately, "Beth, I refuse to talk about this anymore now. You are as white as a ghost." She opened her mouth, but he said sternly without looking at her, "If you have a relapse, I am not sure that I will be able to look Dr. Cotter in the eye. He already does not think I can be much of a husband because I let my wife get in such a state."

To Beth's dismay, William's face had assumed that expressionless mask she had grown to detest and dread. It was more and more apparent that too many things had happened all those years ago that she had not been aware of.

Suddenly the desire to reach up and pull his face down, to touch his lips with her own as she had so delighted to do after they had been first married, almost overwhelmed her. But it had been so long now since they had kissed as lovers. Too long. Fear of his rejection made her close her eyes tightly, clench her hands together to stop them from reaching out to him, clinging to him longer.

She felt him pull up the blankets over her in swift, jerky movements. Then she felt the unexpected, soft touch of his firm lips on her brow, but by the time her eyes had flown open he had already turned away.

By the rigid set of his shoulders as he made for the door without once looking back, she knew she would be wasting her voice trying to tell him he was wrong not to talk it all out now, wrong not to grasp the opportunity to get rid of the poison that had caused so much heartbreak.

She had to know, needed to know all that had happened, all he was thinking. Otherwise, she was dreadfully afraid that any chance for them to have a healthy, happy marriage would be gone forever.

ten

Although she did remain in bed for some time after William left the room, Beth's turmoil of mind was not conducive to having the rest he had commanded.

Her mind went over and over all that had been said. Her heart cried out, *O God, O God what should I do? Help me!* At last, with grim determination, she rose, tidied herself swiftly, and made for the new addition to the house where she knew Elizabeth and John had their room.

"Beth! You should still be resting," Elizabeth exclaimed when she opened the door in answer to Beth's knock.

"Is John with you?" When Elizabeth hesitated, she said pleadingly, "I will be able to rest after you both leave, but I do need to speak to you both now."

Before Elizabeth could speak, John's voice said from behind her, "Let her come in, Elizabeth. You said yourself how much better she has been today, and we do have such little time left."

However, to her disgust, they firmly insisted she sit propped up by pillows up on their bed, pushing aside their belongings they had obviously been packing to make room for her. When they had stopped fussing at last, they sat silently watching her, waiting for her to say what was on her mind, and suddenly Beth was bereft of all the words that had been bubbling up in her as she had made her way to see them.

At last she sat forward and said hesitantly, "John, you. . . William did not give you a chance to say anything after I. . . after I. . ."

Understanding suddenly softened his face. He said softly, "Oh, Beth, are you worrying whether or not I believe you ever received those messages from me?"

She nodded miserably, and Elizabeth gave a small murmur of protest. John smiled at her gently and then looked compassionately back at Beth. "Be assured I. . .we do most certainly believe you," he said gently. "Elizabeth and I have been talking about it all. It is obvious that somehow Percy must have found out who I was."

His face hardened as he continued. "Perhaps I had not hidden my father's letters to my mother as well as I thought I had when I was staying at the Macallisters. Their daughter Penny sometimes cleaned out my room. We think she may have found them and read enough to at least tell Percival."

"Tell Percy?" Beth asked with a puzzled frown. "But why would she do that? I was not even aware she knew him, and he was always so above himself he hardly spoke to the servants at Fleetwood, let alone speaking to a gamekeeper's daughter."

John gave a dry laugh. "But then, the servants at Fleetwood were not as beautiful as young Penny Macallister."

Beth's eyes widened. "Oh."

"And from what you have said," Elizabeth added, "she would have been glad to get back at the most handsome man in the county for not taking any notice of her, especially when he started showing any interest in another woman."

John grinned at her. "Perhaps," he conceded, and then became grave again. "Percival Farnley told us that it was Penny who had taken my packet of papers and given them to my. . .my father, so she must have removed them from beneath the loose floorboard in my room before my lawyers looked for them when I was trying to prove my identity."

"Or," Beth said slowly, "her mother may have. She was apparently convinced you had killed her husband and became very bitter. But at least when her mother died, Penny did the decent thing and took the papers to Father."

"If they looked for them at all," Elizabeth said in a thoughtful voice.

They both looked at her, wondering what she meant

Comprehension dawned on John first. "You think the lawyers only told Judge Wedgewood the papers could not be found, further proving me a liar?" he asked sharply.

"Well, you did tell me once it had been Percy who had been so kind to you from the start, telling you he was acting on Lord Farnley's behalf, that he did not doubt for a moment that you were innocent. And wasn't it he who employed the lawyers for you in the first place?"

John swept his hand through his black hair in a gesture that brought back vivid memories to Beth of a boy and girl innocently enjoying themselves in a flower-strewn meadow. Pain lashed through her. The boy was long gone, and she? There were some days she could hardly believe she had ever been young.

"So this is where you are?" a furious voice said from the open doorway.

"Oops!" John muttered, and Elizabeth stifled a smile.

Beth looked at William's angry, white face with trepidation. But she lifted her chin gamely and said steadily, "There were things I had to know."

"But surely—"

"Oh, come and sit down with us, William, and stop babying her," Elizabeth interrupted impatiently.

Beth glanced at her with some surprise. Until that moment, she had only seen Elizabeth as the embodiment of patience.

William hesitated, and Beth said coaxingly, "Please, William, I did rest for awhile, but we do need to find out what happened when Jock was killed, and also all about Kate and Adam."

John looked from William back to Beth and said gently, "William and I have spent a lot of time together while you have been ill. He can tell you some other time what I have already told him about my good friend Adam and your. . .our sister's adventures."

He gave an incredulous laugh, his eyes sparkling brightly. "Oh, you don't know how good it is to say that, to know I do have a loving family. All my life, the only relatives I thought I had were a taciturn, hateful grandfather and uncles and cousins who made my life an absolute torment because of my English ancestry."

"So all you told me about living with your Spanish relatives was true, John?" Beth asked quietly. "Even to your looking for your English father?"

Compassion filled his eyes. "I never lied to you, Beth, I just never told you who my father was and that I was only there working at Fleetwood to try and find out what kind of man he was and how best to approach him."

She surveyed him thoughtfully, and then smiled slightly, "And also befriending me to ask me all those questions about him."

He colored slightly and gave a light, apologetic grimace.

"There is one thing you have never told me." William interrupted their exchange a little harshly. "Do you have any idea why Percy killed old Jock?"

John's expression hardened to flint. He glanced at Elizabeth and then Beth before saying, "Shall we just leave it that we think Jock may have challenged him belligerently about his relationship with his daughter, who after all was even younger than Beth. Percy would have considered that an insult, a challenge to his position as the future Lord Farnley. I think that had become an obsession with him, especially if we are right in thinking he knew or guessed who I was."

He stopped and then added thoughtfully, "I wonder if his father, my uncle, knew about the marriage to my mother. He would certainly have told his son, and when I arrived with my Spanish complexion and the family's unmistakable blue eyes . . . That was why I made sure I never actually met my father."

He shrugged sadly. "I don't suppose now we will ever know, but whatever did happen, Kate and I both agree that Percy must have been mentally unstable even then. As I told you, he was absolutely insane when he confronted us that day. . .that day. . ."

He stopped abruptly, and it was Elizabeth who said firmly, "And we have decided not to talk about that horrible day anymore. It just makes it harder for us. . ." She drew a deep breath and continued. "Harder for me, at least, to forgive him as God wants me to for all he did and tried to do."

Beth looked at her curiously. Forgive a man like Percival Farnley? A murderer, a man who had been responsible for so much misery? Was that possible? She glanced across at William. He was nodding slightly in understanding and looking sympathetically at Elizabeth and John as though he fully acknowledged what she was saying.

He turned and caught her watching him. His face stiffened, and he said at once, "Well, Beth, is that all you need to know right at this moment? I went to your room to find you and tell you Lucy has food ready for us. She has set a place for you and will be very disappointed if you do not put in an appearance in the dining room."

She stared at him. Desperately, she wanted to ask if he had mentioned anything to their guests about his misapprehension of her and John's relationship. Something of her thoughts must have appeared in her face, for his eyes narrowed, and he shook his head ever so slightly as he stood up quickly and held out his hand commandingly to her. "Come on, Mrs. Garrett, it's time you took your seat at our table with our guests."

She hesitated and then gave in gracefully, accepting his hand and letting him lead the way to their luncheon.

The rest of the day flew by. Beth deeply regretted the amount of time she had wasted hiding away in her room as the four of them spent the remainder of their time together creating bonds of love and friendship that she knew would last through time and distance.

It thrilled her to see that John and William so obviously had become good friends. John was very different from the intense, sometimes bitter young man she had befriended years before. Despite all he had been through, he had an inner peace and joy that she envied, and rather to her surprise, she could not but help feel a tinge of jealousy at the way the other three spoke so easily and naturally about their faith in Christ.

It had never been easy for her to talk about church and religion, but the others had a common rapport that made her realize how little she and William really discussed spiritual things outside of church affairs. As she watched and listened, she suddenly felt a deep hunger to somehow also find this personal relationship with God.

The next morning, William was to drive Elizabeth and John to their ship. Beth deeply regretted not yet being strong enough to survive the drive to Port Adelaide where their ship was waiting, even though the new carriage William had purchased was well-sprung and so different from the old cart that had carried her that Sunday when James had been in such a hurry to arrive.

They left early, and after last hugs and fond farewells, Beth waved good-bye until they disappeared from sight. With tears in her eyes, she wondered if she would ever see them again. From several things William had said the evening before, she knew that he was becoming more and more committed to staying in South Australia, and she was not at all sure how she felt about that now.

It was almost dark by the time she heard the carriage returning. Throughout the day, although she still had to take regular periods of rest, she had once again taken up the reins of ordering her household. But the more she realized all that would need to be done, the more concerned she became. As the children grew older and their demands increased, how would she manage properly with just Lucy to help? Single, unattached women with no family were not permitted to settle here, and as they had discovered when trying to find servants, those who were part of a family already had more than enough to do helping their own.

As the hours had passed and William had not returned,

Beth's agitation about how they would be able to relate without the buffer of Elizabeth and John increased. Would the old barriers still be there? Despite her fears, her heart leaped with relief and pleasure when she heard his familiar step and voice at long last. She hurried to meet him, and then stopped in surprise at the sight of his companions.

William came toward her, a beaming smile on his face. "How do you like my surprise, Beth?" He waved his hands towards the two women standing in the hallway. "Please come and meet Mrs. MacGregor, our new housekeeper, and Miss Fisher, our nurse for the children."

"William!" Beth exclaimed with delight.

Stepping past him she shook both women by the hand. They looked surprised and then gratified at her sincere welcome. Mrs. MacGregor was a rather stout, middle-aged woman and answered in a soft, Scottish voice. Miss Fisher was considerably older than Beth, but still blushed as she murmured in response and bobbed a shy curtsy.

"But how. . . ? Where have you come from?" Beth laughed at the amazement on each face as they looked at each other. "Oh, I am so sorry, it is just that we have tried and tried to get someone willing to come out here and work. I am so pleased, and I do hope you will be happy with us," she added a little more subdued, suddenly realizing this might not be the most mature way for the mistress of the house to welcome the servants!

After they had been assigned a room in the addition to the house only vacated that morning by Elizabeth and John, Beth left them to their unpacking and bustled off to get Lucy to prepare supper for them. But Lucy greeted her with a beaming smile and the information that the situation was all under control because the Reverend had let her into the secret before he had left that morning.

"Said he interviewed them yesterday when he was in town with Lord Farnley. That's why I was so insistent I did out those rooms today and not tomorrow, ma'am," she beamed.

"Reverend Garrett had ordered me to already, like."

"Oh, did he just?" Beth said with a smile and hurried to find the miscreant.

All thought of any constraint between them was gone as she rushed into his study babbling out, "Oh, William, they both seem so nice. However did you find them, you clever, clever man?"

Without thinking, she rushed up to him, and it seemed so perfectly natural when his arms came out for her to fling herself into them. His arms closed around her as they had so many times over the years, and with a sigh of pleasure she hugged him enthusiastically.

Then she pushed back slightly to look up into his face, still bubbling over with delight and relief, saying, "I realized today as never before how much more work there is now, especially with the house so much bigger and James showing us it will not be long at all before he is on the move, and now you have solved our problems, and. . ."

She stilled. He was looking down at her in bemusement, as though she was not real, a figment of his imagination. And the past was there between them again. She started to pull back, but his arms tightened convulsively, not letting her go.

"Oh, Beth, Beth," he choked and rested his head against hers. "It has been so long, so long since you came into my arms like that."

It was the feel of his big, strong body trembling against her that dissolved all her stiffness. Her body melted against his, pressing even closer, reveling in his touch, the familiar fragrance of him. Then he pulled back just enough to search out her lips, and she lifted her own to meet his with a sigh of relief.

The kiss seemed to go on forever, time meaning nothing as two hearts strove toward each other.

"Farva? You home, now?"

There was a squeal of delight, and a little body barreled into them.

Beth winced as he jarred her still-tender leg. William let her go and grabbed at his small son. "Oops there, don't hurt Mother's sore leg, you young fiend."

He swung Harold up into his arms, returned his enthusiastic hug, and then looked at Beth from dark, glowing eyes. His whole face was alight with that smile she loved so much, and which had been missing for so long.

"A man should go away all day every day for a welcome like this when he gets home," he said in a husky, delighted voice.

Beth felt the heat mount up in her face. "Don't you dare!" she threatened, and then, despite her effort to control it, her voice cracked as she said, "I don't want you away for a moment longer than you have to be, and. . .and I don't think my heart. . .my heart could stand it either."

It was his turn to color up, but wordlessly, he reached out and brought her up against him again, Harold squeezed in between them. His embrace lasted far too short a moment for her, because Harold squealed with delight and flung an arm around each of their necks and hugged them enthusiastically.

At the same time, Lucy's happy voice said primly from behind them, "If you please, supper is ready."

A laugh rumbled through William's chest, and he whispered in Beth's ear, "If we want fewer interruptions, it is even more a blessing to now have a housekeeper who may hopefully be a little more successful in training Lucy to be more circumspect in interrupting the master and mistress of the house at such moments!"

He let her go, and she looked at him reproachfully, feeling incredibly embarrassed as she saw their new housekeeper peering curiously over Lucy's shoulder.

William watched her red face with delight and grinned unrepentantly. She flashed him a look that made him laugh out loud.

She drew herself up and, with her nose in the air as befitting the stepdaughter of a lord, said regally, "Thank you, Lucy," as though what Mrs. MacGregor had just seen was something she could either like or get used to.

Despite Beth's invitation to join them, Mrs. MacGregor insisted in her soft Scottish voice they would take their meals with Lucy in the kitchen. She calmly bore both the just-arrived nurse and Lucy off so firmly that William looked at Beth and laughed.

"Her husband died earlier this year and left her practically destitute. Only her married daughter came out from Scotland with them, and she told me straight out she preferred to work for strangers for money than be an unpaid skivvy for her lazy daughter. Miss Fisher expressed similar sentiments about her brother's brood."

As he escorted her to the dining room, he added reverently, "As He has promised, the Lord has met our needs once more."

Beth smilingly agreed, and immediately thought of that even deeper need she had. Was William right? It seemed to work for him. God did seem to answer his prayers, but could she dare to tell Him her desires? As she smiled and enjoyed their meal, thankful the constraint between them was not as she had feared it might be, she wondered if God could possibly make William return her love, care for her even a fraction as much as she loved him.

After the household had settled for the night, William sat for a long time outside in the darkness. Beth had already murmured her good night and slipped away to her room. He had been uncertain what else to say to her.

Would she welcome him if he dared to join her?

He had felt a tremendous wave of relief when John and Elizabeth had told him Beth had not even known she had pushed him away, rejected him so cruelly when she had been ill. But all day he had been wondering if it had only been the fever speaking. Had it been that only in her delirium was she able to voice her true feelings toward him?

If she rebuffed him now, it would hurt so very, very much. More than he dared think about. He did not want to put her in the position of asking him to leave. It could harm the very tentative green shoots of a new, deeper relationship that he longed for with her.

In the end, she had looked so pale and weary, he had let her go to her room with only a brief kiss good night on her cheek. There would be another day, another time, he had tried to tell himself.

But now he was feeling so lonely, wondering what he should do. It was a warm evening, and he studied the bright stars as he often liked to do, trying to find the constellation that had been pointed out to him as the Southern Cross.

"Well, Lord," he murmured, still looking up toward the twinkling canopy of stars, "thank You for this good day. Thank You for leading me to our two badly needed servants. Thank You for the time with John and Elizabeth. Thank You that he is such a fine brother in Christ it was easy to love him after all. Thank You for his faith in You and the mutual fellowship in You that I enjoyed so much."

He paused and dropped his head. "And now, Lord, please. . . please give me wisdom about what to do, what to say to Beth."

He was still for another long moment, and then with a heartfelt groan he spoke quickly, his voice rising in his pain. "I know I should never have married her the way I did. I am so very sorry for not seeking Your will back then, for not talking to her before about the whole mess. But we are husband and wife. It is done, and now how to go back to what we had before? Does she want to still be my wife? How can I. . .?"

There was a movement behind him, and he swung sharply around.

A soft, trembling voice said out of the darkness, "Why don't you just ask her, William?"

He sprang to his feet. And was struck dumb.

In the dim light of the lamp she held, he could see she was

wearing nothing but a silky nightdress. She was very still, and then at long last, while he was still trying to find his voice, she took a slow, hesitant step forward. A gentle breeze lifted the gossamer-like folds of fabric around her ankles and bare feet. They came alive, shimmering and dancing in the flickering light.

Suddenly he remembered. They were the same enticing nightclothes she had worn that very first night. Their wedding night.

"Elizabeth said. . .she said. . .oh, William, I am so sorry I was so horrible and nasty to you when I was sick. I did not mean it, William. How could I possibly not want my old friend and protector near me?"

He heard the tears in her voice, and his heart trembled even more. He opened his mouth, but the words were tumbling from her as though she was afraid she might lose her courage.

"I have been so lonely in bed all by myself. oh, William, it has been so for many, many months. Now you know. . .you know that what you thought wasn't so. . .can you bear to share it with me again?"

There was a pleading in her soft, almost incoherent whisper that broke his heart, that kept him speechless even as he stepped forward and enfolded her in his arms.

She held herself rigidly for a moment, until with a shuddering sigh she at last melted against him as she had a few hours before. And he knew his lonely bed would be so no longer.

As Beth felt William's arms holding her close, she sighed with the most profound relief. She had been so scared, so afraid as she had waited for him, hoping against hope that he would come to her.

But she knew him well enough to know how hurt he would have been when he had heard her ban him from her sickroom, even if she had been delirious at the time. What he would have thought, his pain and humiliation in front of John and Elizabeth had been haunting her dreadfully.

At last she had known this was all she could do to try and make up to him for the dreadful anguish Elizabeth had told her he had been through. But, as she felt his arms close around her, as she held him close, as he carried her to their bedroom, she knew this was only the beginning of sorting out all that was between them.

He kissed her gently, tenderly said he loved her as he had told her so many times before. But as before, she knew it was still only the love he had felt for her since she had been a child.

Long after he had fallen asleep she stared wistfully into the darkness above their bed. She was happier, more at peace than she had been for a long time. And yet she wished fervently that there could be more. More than respect and friendship. More than the shared love of her childish days.

She wished he could love her as she loved him. With that once-in-a-lifetime, God-given love between a man and woman.

eleven

As the days and then the months slipped by, the household settled down. Mrs. MacGregor and Miss Fisher proved to be the treasures William and Beth had hoped. Harold and James took to their nurse straightaway.

Beth, used to the servants at Fleetwood and their London church house, was amazed but absolutely delighted with Mrs. MacGregor. That resourceful, hardworking woman willingly turned her hand to anything that needed doing, from cleaning and laundry to even helping in the large vegetable garden, declaring she loved the excuse to be outdoors. Lucy bloomed as a cook under the experienced woman's tutelage.

Henry Wild, a strange, silent little man, was added to the household. He claimed to have been working for some years in New South Wales, but William suspected at least some of those years may have been as a convict.

However, he had looked William straight in the eye with a fierce look of pride mixed with such desperate hope that William had given him a job, and not for a moment had he regretted the decision. Henry rarely spoke about himself but proved to know a great deal about farming and worked for long hours in the fields—or paddocks, as they were told was the more popular term. Things progressed so well, William even bought adjoining acreage lots as they were released.

William had at last managed to purchase a couple more horses—a scarce commodity in South Australia—to help with the plowing. Poultry was added to the farmyard as well as a couple extra cows. Harold took great pride in helping to feed the "hickins" and find their nests where the eggs were laid. Some fences of rough branches and scrub had been erected to keep the animals away from the vegetable garden, and more were under construction around the small wheat crop William had managed to plant earlier in the year with help from Robert Young.

Life was so hectic, there were times when William and Beth marveled at how some assisted emigrants managed with no money to hire help and purchase items that made life easier. As a result, once their more urgent needs had been met, Henry found himself several times working side by side with William on neighboring properties, taking their horse and plow to turn over virgin ground and clear stumps, fencing, even helping to build the primitive wattle and daub huts which was all many settlers could afford.

And of course the women were there also. Sometimes Mrs. MacGregor and Lucy even swung a hoe or digging fork to help establish a vegetable garden for a new, often bewildered and overworked settler's wife. More than once some poor sick woman or new mother would find her piles of laundry done or baskets of prepared food left to tide the family over.

Although it was essential William took care of the immediate and future physical well-being of those in his household, he believed more than ever that he was called to be a minister of the gospel. Each day immediately after breakfast, he insisted that everyone gather for prayer and a short reading of the Scriptures.

Henry had at first strongly resisted, but when he discovered his continuing employment depended on his attendance, he had sat glowering through each session. To William's gratification and Beth's relief, Henry's attitude was gradually softening, even to the extent of voluntarily starting to attend the church services. People of all persuasions enjoyed the fellowship, teaching from the Scriptures, and worship. Somewhat to William's bemusement, there were Primitive Methodists, Wesleyans, Scotch Baptists, Presbyterians, Congregationalists, and others. Of course it did lead to some interesting debates at times, which William enjoyed immensely.

At the insistence of the community, William continued to organize the services each month, although as the numbers increased Beth had suggested they should be held more often. She even ventured to suggest that some building be erected to hold them in.

"More and more settlers are moving into this area," she had argued after the last meeting, "and none of us like having to travel every other Sunday all the way to the services in the center of Adelaide. If the numbers keep increasing, that old sail shelter will never do on days of bad weather, even for these sturdy, faithful people."

But the last week or so, William had gradually become more concerned about Beth, and this last day or so his concern had increased. For weeks after Elizabeth and John had left, she had seemed happier than she had for a long time. Occasionally he thought he saw a fleeting look of sadness in her eyes he could not understand. As soon as she realized he was watching her, she would smile at him so quickly that he decided he must be mistaken.

They had gradually reverted back to the easy friendship they had known for so many years before their marriage, and if he longed sometimes quite desperately for there to be more, he managed to hide it. Or he hoped he had.

In those first few weeks his hopes had been high that she might grow to love him as he had prayed she would ever since she had been sixteen. But gradually that hope was once again fading, and now he realized how much she had again lost her sparkle. She was quieter, her smile coming less spontaneously, and sometimes he had caught her staring into the distance with a strange look on her face he could not fathom.

Of course, spring in this Great Southland had proven much warmer then those spring days in Yorkshire, where the snow would ever so slowly melt away and allow the daffodils to poke their heads up. Now in early December, the days had become very dry and hot, reminding them that in this upside-down country, Christmas would be celebrated in the heat of summer.

Beth had very quickly regained her full strength, organizing the household and family affairs efficiently, supporting him fully with the church services and other areas of ministry. More demands were coming for visits to individuals for spiritual counseling, and William knew God had provided Henry at just the right time to free him up to minister to those in need.

But he had been reluctant to put more pressure on Beth. The folk who came to the services had got into the habit of sharing a picnic lunch together. Since that first service they now always brought their own food, but he knew it inevitably did mean extra work for Beth and their servants, even though he did his utmost to help, especially if the weather turned nasty and everyone had to cram indoors.

He tried to think of anything that may have upset her. Mrs. MacGregor and Miss Fisher were working out very well, so it was not them. The children were thriving. Beth always greeted him just as warmly as ever when he returned home after being away all day.

More of his time was being taken up visiting those in need. On many occasions Beth joined him on those visits and displayed a sensitivity and caring that soon made her a very welcome guest indeed. Never did they go empty-handed. Whether it be fresh vegetables, a pot of soup for a family with a sick mother, or something as simple as a batch of scones to share with busy parents over a quick cup of tea, it always seemed to be the appropriate thing to ease his way, to help break down any barriers so he could minister to other, deeper needs of the mind and heart.

Sometimes he even wondered if Beth was not trying just a little too hard to be a good minister's wife. And then one day he received news he had been waiting anxiously for.

"Beth, how would you like a few hours in Adelaide with

me?" he asked her that evening. "We will leave the children with Miss Fisher. I am sure there is much we must need to purchase in preparation for Christmas."

To his concern, a look of dismay touched her face briefly. She usually jumped at any chance for one of their rare outings to the shops.

But then to his immense relief, she said, "There are quite a few things we need, including some special gifts for Christmas." She frowned and added quickly, "In fact, Miss Fisher told me today we simply must have more material for clothes for the boys. They are both growing so fast. It was then I told her William Pedler made those beautiful little shoes for Harold, and she became very keen to have her own replaced by him. I ended up promising her she could have tomorrow off."

He felt annoyed and knew it sounded in his voice as he said shortly, "It would have been best to have mentioned it to me first. I'm afraid tomorrow is the only day I can spare. We start to harvest our meager crop of wheat any day now. Miss Fisher will have to go another time."

Beth scowled at him and opened her mouth to argue. To his relief she changed her mind and smiled reluctantly before saying feelingly, "As long as you are the one to tell her so. I hate to disappoint her. She was so excited."

Early the next morning, Beth sat beside William as he tooled the carriage down the rough and narrow track toward the main road to Adelaide. Despite her discomfort, she felt a thrill of pleasure to know they would be spending the whole day by themselves. There was a suppressed air of excitement about William, and she was delighted that he, too, was so looking forward to their day together. He had braved Miss Fisher's displeasure and even refused Henry's offer to drive the carriage.

"I still don't know why you insisted on bringing this huge thing instead of our smaller one," Beth grumbled mildly as the carriage lurched and creaked its way onto the slightly wider but still rough main road.

"But think how many more parcels it will hold, my dear wife," William answered lightly.

A pang shot through Beth at his light endearment, but she grinned up at him. "More like to hold more bags of seeds for your precious garden," she teased.

He grinned back at her and turned his attention back to the two eager, fresh horses now trotting swiftly along the wider road that wound down from the foothills where they had their property. They chatted casually about various things until the dwelling places were closer together and more areas of bush had been cleared and the land cultivated.

Looking around at the few tired-looking wheat paddocks they sped past, William frowned as he said briefly, "It is still very dry here despite the rain we had a couple weeks ago. Even drier than where we are closer to the mountains."

"Mrs. MacGregor said her daughter told her when she visited her yesterday that they heard from some new arrivals that the drought in New South Wales was so severe that the governor of New South Wales, Sir George Gibbs, had called the nation to prayer," Beth said softly.

"Yes," William said slowly, "she told me also. Apparently he proclaimed last November second a day of fasting and humiliation throughout the whole land, right down to Melbourne."

Beth was silent. She saw William glance at her, and she turned and watched his face as she said slowly, "Did she also tell you that within two days heavy rain began to fall?"

"Yes, she did."

He smiled at her, and after a moment she smiled back, but then said softly, a little shyly, "God does care, doesn't He?"

"Oh, yes," William said fervently, "and I am so thankful He cares just as much about the small things as the big ones in our lives."

She hesitated, wishing she could speak as easily about Almighty God as William could, wondering if this was the moment she should ask him the question that had been troubling her so in recent months. Why did she not have any-where near the same closeness with God that he had? She had worked so hard trying to be good, especially these last months.

All she had been assured of was that at the very least she was a virtuous woman as the verse in Proverbs urged her to be. She loved William so much she would be a "crown to her hus-band" and not "rottenness in his bones" if it killed her!

But despite all her efforts, God did not always seem real to her. During their short visit, it had been so very obvious that Elizabeth and John also had that something extra in their rela-tionship with God that William had. There had been times Beth had listened quietly as the three had talked about Jesus and spiritual matters as though He were so real He was in the room with them. Why did she not have that same easy relationship with God they seemed to have?

Once again she hesitated too long. The traffic had increased a great deal, too much for them to engage in a serious discus-sion, and William had to concentrate as he drove through the increasingly congested streets to the heart of the city. After a few moments, William pulled the carriage to a stop, and Beth was pleased to see they were outside the shoemaker's premises in Leigh Street.

As William fixed the brake, a young lad raced out to hold the horses' heads for him.

"Why, thank you kindly, young William the Fourth," he said teasingly to the boy, who grinned and informed him cheerfully in his Cornish accent that he was welcome and his father was at home.

William helped Beth down, saying with the twinkle she loved so much, "Come on, my dearest, this young man's father, William the Third, has been busy on an order for me. I'm glad they are so fond of the name 'William.' It shows very good taste indeed."

As soon as they were out of earshot he murmured, "But I am still very glad we have not burdened our sons like that! Now, we'll have to be quick with this errand, as I have an appointment in Emigration Square very soon."

She glanced at him curiously, wondering again about his suppressed air of excitement and who the appointment could be with. Surely he was not contemplating hiring more help, as she knew he had already organized help from the locals for the harvest in another week or so when their few acres of wheat were completely ready.

Mrs. Elizabeth Pedler greeted them cheerfully as they entered the small workshop at the front of their primitive mud hut. Beth remembered the story of Mrs. Pedler's first harsh night at Holdfast Bay, and as she looked at the woman's pale, tired-looking face, she knew the Pedlers' fifth child would arrive the following year.

Mrs. Pedler confirmed Beth's assessment with a grimace as she saw her guest's comprehensive glance. "Next May or June," she said bluntly, adding proudly, "and the first Pedler born here in South Australia." She smiled briefly. "I do hope William has finished your work boots, Reverend Garrett. He is very excited because his brother Thomas has decided to join him and his other two brothers, Joseph and James, out here. A decision rather forced on him I'm afraid, because he has faced very strong opposition to the new machinery he installed at his shoemaking business in Falmouth." She gave a wry smile and added, "The usual story—the people objecting to losing their jobs destroy the business."

William smiled easily as she sent her solemn little son Darius to find his father. "I am sure his shoemaking skills will be put to very good use out here. By the way, I have heard that your brother-in-law Joseph is involved in digging wells. I would be very much obliged if you would tell him I have decided to add another one to our property."

Beth stared at William, a little peeved that he had not mentioned this to her beforehand. In the beginning they had discussed everything to do with their new home.

"I thought too many wells in our area contained water that was too brackish," she commented later as they walked toward Emigration Square.

"I thought of trying again in the paddock right next to the house," he said in such an absentminded voice that she glanced at him sharply. He was peering around at the passing crowd eagerly, as though searching for a familiar face.

"Just who are we meeting here, William?" she asked curiously, glancing around herself.

Several feet away, a tall woman wearing a very modish bonnet stood with her back to them. She was also looking around at the crowd. Beth's glance lingered for a moment on the very pretty bonnet, and then something about the woman reminded her of Kate. The woman turned her head and stared straight at her.

For a moment Beth thought she was dreaming. Then the woman's face lit up in a radiant, familiar smile. It was Kate!

Her hand tucked into William's elbow tightened convulsively. Even as he swung around, she gave a breathless gasp and then was flying toward Kate, into her arms to laugh and cry and exclaim over and over at seeing her dearly loved sister again.

twelve

"But how. . .when. . .what are you doing here?" Beth exclaimed between hugs and tears of delight.

"We came by ship, which anchored yesterday, and we are here because Kate could not bear another moment without seeing her sister," a deep, amused voice said from behind her.

Adam Stevens was shaking a radiant William's hand. Kate disentangled herself from Beth's arms and held out her hand to Adam. For a fleeting moment, Beth had an image of John doing a similar thing to Elizabeth. The Farnley blue eyes were flashing with the same excitement and pride as Kate said with a loving smile, "Beth, I believe you received my letter with our news?"

Impulsively, Beth stepped forward and flung her arms around Adam. She gave him a swift kiss on the cheek and then stood back and beamed at them both as she said, "Oh, I was so very pleased for you both, but how dared you get married without me, Kate!"

She gave Kate a cheeky grin, and added, "Let me tell you, I was not oversurprised. I saw on board ship how it was with both of you, and I am so very glad you have realized you were meant for each other."

Adam stared at her, and then he looked quickly at Kate. "So you were right. Beth does not miss much."

Kate laughed at him and then held out her hand to William. "And how is my favorite brother-in-law? Still trying to keep this minx in order, I hope?" Her smile died a little, and she glanced quickly from him to Beth. "I do hope you are fully recovered now, Beth, my dear," she added a little anxiously. "Elizabeth and John were very worried about you."

"They wrote to you?" Beth felt something like disappointment, which was entirely stupid, of course. For one moment she had thought William must have asked them to come as a special treat for her for on their first Christmas in Australia.

But then Adam chuckled and said indulgently, "Getting John's letter was bad enough for Kate, but when William's letter arrived there was no stopping her from agreeing to his pleading to spend Christmas with you."

Suddenly Beth's heart was singing again. She beamed at William, delighted to see the telltale touch of color stain his face. "And I suppose you let poor Miss Fisher into the secret of your surprise and that was why she was so amazingly complacent about you imperiously delaying her day off!"

The use of the large carriage was also explained when they loaded it with the huge amount of baggage and boxes that had accompanied the two travelers.

"No, no, we have not come to stay any longer than into the new year," laughed Kate as she saw Beth surveying all their belongings with considerable awe. "But it will soon be Christmas," she teased, "and I know how much you have always enjoyed opening presents, Beth darling."

Beth felt the smallest trace of irritation. That had certainly been true when she had been younger. Now she enjoyed giving even more than opening her own presents, had, in fact, for the last three years. Would Kate and William never stop thinking of her as a child? Feeling dreadfully guilty at the thought, she gave Kate an extra hug in silent apology for being so ungrateful.

Beth certainly did thoroughly enjoy the weeks leading up to Christmas. The days took on an excitement that she could never quite remember being as intense at Fleetwood. There were moments of nostalgia—as when the men brought in some pieces of green leaves and tied them in strategic places, claiming they were as close to mistletoe as they could find amid the eucalyptus trees. But although the leaves produced the same sneaked kisses and although the huge plum pudding carried in by a beaming Lucy on Christmas Day was from the same recipe Kate had had the cook use at Fleetwood, it was still not the same, still not at all like Christmas without the snow and cold of England.

Yet there was a closeness between the colonists that gathered for the early morning Christmas Day service that Beth could not remember among the folk on the estate in Yorkshire. Here there was so little of the class distinction that had inevitably been part of past celebrations of the Savior's birth.

She and William smiled at each other in understanding as at one stage they saw Adam and Henry in deep conversation. Both were ex-convicts, although Beth strongly suspected Henry's sentence had been for crimes he had committed, whereas Adam had told William about his taking the blame and punishment for his younger, weaker brother's embezzlement of family money.

There was no doubt in either William or Beth's mind that Adam and Kate were blissfully happy together. They spoke eagerly of their new home at Waverley over the huge mountain range west of Sydney and of their good friends the Hardy family, now managing Adam's other sheep property, Stevens' Downs, a few hundred miles farther west. They told of the limited success they were having in getting to know the language and ways of the local aboriginals and their attempts to care for them.

Both Adam and Kate were extremely interested in Beth's account of the aboriginal woman who had helped her find Harold.

"And you say you have not seen any sign of aboriginals near here since?" Kate asked Beth with some disappointment.

Before she could answer, William said swiftly, "As a matter of fact, I was told only the other day that they seem to have returned and have established a small camp in the hills near the water hole several miles back."

"Why, William," Beth said with excitement, "perhaps we can go and find that woman and her child, after all."

William looked cautious. "Perhaps," he said flatly, "but only if we make sure it is safe to do so."

"And perhaps she may not want to be found," Kate said quietly. "They are usually very independent and self-reliant unless good-meaning white people mess them up."

Adam looked grim and said shortly, "The local people in our area have been given too much alcohol by unthinking settlers, and it is breaking our hearts to see what this is doing to many fine aboriginals."

"But Jackie is standing out against it," Kate said with a fond smile, and then had to tell them about the aboriginal reared and educated by white missionaries in the Hunter Valley, who had helped them so much when they had been in danger from Percival Farnley.

"I heard that some men have recently been brought to trial for murdering aboriginals at Myall Creek, west of Tamworth in northwest New South Wales," William said gravely.

Kate shuddered. "That massacre of twenty-five men, women, and children in June was absolutely appalling, although apparently it is by no means the first time aboriginals have been killed with virtually no action taken against their murderers by the authorities."

"And even sadder was the fact that this particular group was peaceful and had not caused any of the troubles others had. Unfortunately they were the only ones the revengeful stockmen could find," Adam said grimly. Then he added slowly, "Of course, in all fairness to the white people on isolated stations, they were becoming completely demoralized and scared out of their wits by the constant harassment and attacks by some aboriginals. They were further upset because the promised mounted police were suddenly called away to other troubled areas. But there can never be any real excuse for killing innocent aboriginals like that," he concluded sadly.

"The report said some squatters in particular are very opposed to the trial of the men responsible and are raising money for their defense," William said quietly, looking curiously at Adam. "I heard that the station superintendent who reported it to the government and acted as a witness at the trial lost his job because of it."

Adam shrugged. "Well, I am not one of those squatters, but the argument has certainly divided the country. The men were acquitted at their trial, but last we heard a new trial has been set, and I doubt they will escape the hangman this time round."

He hesitated before adding slowly, "As I said, I can sympathize a little with those in areas where the aboriginals have been causing trouble. Some have had their workers at outstations, both men and women, killed. And the number of stock being killed by the aboriginals has risen sharply. Quite a few seem to prefer taking sheep and cattle for food rather than hunting for kangaroos, especially during periods of drought."

Adam sighed. "There is no easy answer, but the problem is that it is still not right to allow any man to take the law into his own hands like those men did. Innocent people may die. It is not just and is certainly not allowed under British law."

William looked at Beth with a worried frown. "It is all beginning to happen here too, Beth, on a lesser scale perhaps, but that is why I want you to always be very careful."

She smiled at him and nodded reassuringly before changing the subject.

With the mixed delights of Christmas behind them, the new year of 1839 commenced with sweltering heat. There were only a few brief thunderstorms, and any moisture quickly dried up. Fortunately the well sunk by Joseph Pedler had yielded a reasonable supply of freshwater, but taking Adam's strong advice, they were very careful not to waste a drop of the precious water they had.

Beth and William took their guests around the new settlement as much as they could and were surprised themselves at the way the number of assisted emigrants were flooding in. Several people were eager to tell them about the German refugees who had arrived in December. They were especially sympathetic toward them when they found out they were Lutherans who had escaped from Prussia and the religious persecution of King Friedrich Wilhelm the Third. Apparently Captain Dirk Hahn of the frigate *Zebra,* on which they had traveled, was so impressed with his passengers that he went out of his way to see them settled on land they could farm.

William had been quiet and thoughtful for some time afterward, and Beth had smiled to herself. She knew it would not be long before he found some way of meeting and offering help to fellow believers who had suffered so much.

Then one day they were introduced to another newly arrived family in the long, rough buildings at Emigration Square. They were about the same age as Adam and Kate, a little older than Beth and William. Francis Telfer was a shepherd from Dumfriesshire in Scotland, and his wife, Jean, and their three young children aged six years and younger had arrived on the *Prince George* on Boxing Day, right after Christmas.

When they wearily, and sometimes with tears, recounted some of what they had experienced, the two couples were reminded vividly of their own unpleasant journey just twelve months before.

Less than four weeks after their application to emigrate, the Telfers had only been given twenty-six days notice that they had been accepted and were due to sail from London the beginning of September. The conditions on board ship had been very crowded, and that combined with the heat and the roll of the ship in turbulent waters had proved too much for their baby boy, John, born just three months before their departure.

"We committed his soul to the Lord and his tiny body to the ocean depths and sailed on," Francis told them gruffly.

Jean gave a small, stifled sob, and Beth was relieved that, as they were leaving, friends the Telfers had made on board ship arrived to help with the children. Dinah Flavel was the same age Beth had been when she had married William but took immediate, capable care of the three small children.

Beth hugged her two healthy sons even tighter that evening after they arrived home, and she shed a few tears as William held her close and said softly, "That poor woman. I fear for her."

Beth did not ask what he meant. She too had quickly noted how frail Jean Telfer had been. She could hardly have recovered from the weakness of childbirth before going through the mental and physical strain of leaving her home. It was to be hoped that the cramped conditions on the ship, the death of her baby, and their arrival with no comforts or conveniences in the midsummer heat would not prove too much for her.

Far too swiftly, Adam and Kate's time with them was drawing to a close. Yet as much as she would have liked to have them nearer, in some strange way, Beth knew that her own roots were growing deeper into this place she could so easily now call home.

Kate and Beth had of course had several long, private discussions. Beth shuddered, and they both shed tears over Percival Farnley and what he had done to John and so nearly done to them all that dreadful, final day in the bush on Waverley.

They all rejoiced together when a letter unexpectedly arrived from their lawyers telling them that despite the initial shock and wariness of the people at Fleetwood, John and Elizabeth were quickly winning the majority over with their love and management of the estate. The letter was full of praise for them both, and the considerable relief of the lawyers that John had at last agreed to be known as John Farnley brought smiles to their faces as well.

Then one day, Beth at last told Kate something that her mother had told her about her new stepfather, insisting she never mention it to Kate.

Kate stared at her in disbelief. "You knew father had been married before he married my mother? Married to someone when he had served with Wellington in Spain? But why did neither he nor my mother ever mention it to me?"

"I do not know," Beth said quietly, "except. . ."

She stopped, reluctant to continue, but after a moment Kate gave a sigh and said sadly what Beth was thinking, "Because it hurt too much to talk about the loss of his first love and their baby son. He never loved my mother like he did yours. And I think he was so unloving toward me because in his own strange way he was still grieving for the son he had never seen and whom he thought had died with his wife. Perhaps it would have been different if I had been another long-desired son."

Beth thought of the anguish on William's face when he thought there might be a chance he would lose claim to Harold, the joy on his face when James had been born. "Poor Father," she whispered.

Beth thought long and hard about telling Kate what William and her father had believed about her and John's relationship, even about Harold. In the end, Beth knew it was still eating into her so much she had to speak of it to someone. She knew she could trust Kate not to mention it to William if she asked her not to, and after the men had gone outside early the morning before Kate and Adam were due to leave, Beth told her step-sister everything.

Kate sat in stunned silence for a long time, staring at Beth with horror. "Now I know why Elizabeth was so concerned about you," she said at last, and when Beth still did not raise her head from staring down at her tightly clenched hands, she whispered, "And how desperately William must have loved you to marry you while believing what Father told him was true."

At that Beth looked up swiftly and said wildly, "Loved me? Loved me! It was Father he loved. Father he wanted to help for all he had done for him over the years."

"Rubbish."

Beth gaped at her, and Kate shook her head at her in disgust. "Really, Beth, certainly you are still very young, even though the mother of two, but when will you grow some sense! William has loved you ever since he first laid eyes on you. And when he returned for your sixteenth birthday, he simply devoured you with his eyes! Even Father commented on it to me."

When Beth continued to gaze at her from dazed eyes, Kate snorted. "Perhaps you think William is a soft touch, lets other people get away with what he has let you get away with over the years. If that is the case, you have not seen him dealing with disobedient servants like I have. Always very firm, very kind, but not giving an inch when he believed he was in the right."

Beth thought of the way he had once dismissed one of their London servants for stealing. Certainly he had tried to help the man when he had been discovered the first time, but he had shown no hint of weakness when he had dismissed him after he had stolen again. Suddenly she remembered other incidents. The way he dealt with unrepentant sinners was always kind, even gentle when necessary, but always very firm. Over and over, William had proven that although he was gentle, he was a strong man in body and spirit.

"And," Kate continued with a decided glint in her eyes, "if you think for one moment he is the sort of soft, spineless man who would marry anyone he did not want to marry, no matter if the queen demanded it of him, well," she concluded with an expressive sweep of her hands, "you are just crazy, my dear. Even now, anyone can tell his face simply lights up whenever you come into a room."

Beth went around in a daze for the rest of the day. Was Kate. . .could Kate possibly be right?

She found herself hardly able to take her eyes off William when they sat down with Adam and Kate for their last evening meal together. She beamed at him when he asked her anxiously if she was feeling all right, simply because she had stared at him without moving when he asked her to pass him the salt. She had been remembering the times in the privacy of their room when he had whispered he loved her, thinking, hoping that if Kate was right, he must have, after all, meant those words the way she wanted him to.

Kate gave a gurgling, choked-off laugh, and to Adam's obvious surprise and bemusement covered it up quickly by launching into some humorous tale of an event involving Jackie and a new chum at Waverley. It turned into a rather involved story of Jackie pretending not to understand a word of English, stringing the poor man along until Adam had been forced to intervene.

Adam took up the story, dryly saying, "Of course, Jackie takes no notice of me whatsoever in that particular area. He just nods in agreement with what I say, grins, and strides away. No doubt he will continue to play his trick on each new white man he meets, backed up of course by the rest of our station hands who think it is a huge joke."

To Beth's frustration no one made any moves to go to bed early, and she was forced to stay up with all of them very late that night. Beth was disappointed when William tugged her into the curve of his body but promptly went to sleep, not giving her a chance to talk to him. In the morning when she woke, he had already gone to help Henry harness the horses to take Kate and Adam to Port Adelaide.

Kate was disgustingly and naughtily amused at Beth's frustration at not being able to talk to William. "Serves you right," she muttered with a heartless chuckle on the way into breakfast, and then laughed out loud at Beth's reproachful look. "I cannot believe you have been married all this time and not known your own husband loves you as much as he does."

"But then, you have not realized how often he has treated me the same as he did when we were children," she burst out in a desperate whisper. As she uttered those words, Beth suddenly knew she was wrong. He had many, many times treated her very much like a woman.

She felt the heat mount up in her face and grinned weakly at Kate when she laughed out loud at her blush. But Kate's amusement quickly changed to concern when Miss Fisher informed them at breakfast that both Harold and James had woke with a slight fever. "Oh, dear," she said, "does that mean you cannot come down to the port to see us off?"

After quickly ascertaining the children were not really ill but decidedly off-color and miserable, Beth swallowed her own disappointment and said with a brave shrug and attempted smile, "It seems I am never fated to be able to wave our family off shipside."

"I could stay with the boys, and you could go, Beth," William said anxiously.

He looked so upset for her that Beth stared at him for a moment and then looked suddenly across at Kate. Her stepsister gave her a knowing "I told you so look," which made Beth suddenly blush a fiery red once again.

"Beth, are you also not feeling well?" William asked in a worried voice. "You look very flushed."

"No, no," she stammered quickly. "I'm fine except for feeling nauseated most mornings," she added without thinking. She jumped to her feet and swiftly followed after Miss Fisher, who had already hurried away again to be with her charges.

For a moment, no one in the room moved. William had half risen from his chair to go after Beth as she exited the room, but then with a stunned look on his face, he sank back into his chair.

Kate gave a wobbly laugh that was almost a sob and said with feeling, "William, I think you may now know the reason Beth has been so pale at times the last few weeks. Believe me, I know how she feels!"

It was Adam's turn to stare at his wife with a puzzled frown. Kate smiled brilliantly at him and jumped to her feet. "Come with me, my darling," she whispered. "There is something I should tell you. Something I was waiting to tell you when we got back to Waverley, but now I find I will burst if I cannot share it with you this minute!"

William stood politely as they left the room, but he ignored Adam's questioning glance, hardly comprehending what Kate meant until a sudden joyful shout of, "Kate, my darling wife!" rang back from the hallway. William smiled for a moment, sharing Adam's wonder and delight at the prospect of being a father in a few months' time.

Then his face creased again in its worried frown. If Beth were pregnant again, why had she not yet told him? A thrill of delight swept through him at the thought of another small baby for them to share, to love. Perhaps a girl this time with golden curls and blue eyes like her beautiful mother.

But then his delight was overshadowed once more by his question. Was Beth, could Beth possibly be worried about what he would say, what he would think? Were the circumstances surrounding Harold's birth still weighing on her mind when he thought they had been at long last laid to rest?

thirteen

Beth waved until the carriage disappeared around the bend. She waited then, cuddling the miserable, teething James in one arm and reaching to hold Harold's little hand tightly, until at last the understanding Catherine Fisher whisked both children away, leaving Beth to wipe at her tears. The carriage appeared again, for a few far-too-brief moments, where the narrow road traveled up the crest of a small hill before once again rolling out of sight.

They were gone, and despite their plans of visiting Adam and Kate at Waverley one day, Beth knew that journey could be a long time in the future.

Before they had bought their property, she and William had both agreed that they would stay in South Australia until the boys were older and it would be safer for them to travel. They were seeing every day how much need there was in this new land for a minister of the gospel.

The decision not to risk traveling with the small children had been confirmed to Beth once again after meeting the Telfers and being reminded of how dangerous even a sea voyage to Sydney could be. And now. . .now there would be another baby to consider.

Once again, she thought of telling William about the baby. She would do so this evening, along with other things she needed to tell him, to ask him! She thrilled at the thought of convincing him of her love for him. Although, now she knew there was really no need to ask him to confirm his love, and she castigated herself for ever doubting someone of his integrity.

Her lips twitched in a rueful smile. She would still need all the strength and patience God could give her once he knew about the baby. Once again she would be fussed over until the Reverend Garrett drove her crazy!

He had paid such detailed attention to her every comfort on the other two occasions she had suffered from the sickness in the mornings that she had decided to put off telling him as long as she could. It had always just seemed one more way William made her feel too young. She, a mother of two children, just hated being treated like a child, even if at times she did act like a foolish one, she acknowledged with a grimace.

But ever since she had talked to Kate, she had looked at William's care of her with new eyes. Always she had bemoaned her short height and slight, fair frame, longing to be tall and strong like Kate. And in all honesty, she had to admit that her seemingly frail appearance did give William every excuse to treat her gently.

But had he really treated her like a child when he had agreed to their long journey to Australia, to their buying their own ten acres and making their home so far from the security of England and any family?

Beth turned and surveyed her domain with sudden pride and satisfaction as never before. Their large, white, stone house with its bark- and brush-covered roof gleamed in the sun. A separate kitchen had been built next to it to protect the main house against kitchen fires. William had only stated a few days ago that their next project should be to replace the roof of the house with neat shingles.

The stables down the slight slope, well away from the house, had been extended, and a couple rooms had been made to give Henry the comfortable accommodation away from the house that the independent loner had said he strongly preferred. The improvements to the cow and poultry sheds and the yards to confine their three horses and two cows had been finished with the expert help of Adam in recent weeks. The large, fenced vegetable garden was between the stables and the house and, to their delight, was now starting to yield produce over and above their own needs so that they could sell or even give it away.

Beth smiled slightly, thinking about the inevitable upheaval that would occur while the roof was being replaced. She started toward the house with a light step. William would always accomplish what he decided should be done. He always had, and he always would.

The sound of a fast-running horse made her pause and swing around. Bob Young came into sight. His grave face worried her, even before he called out to her as he pulled his plunging horse to a stop.

"Hello there, Mrs. Garrett. Is William home?"

"He has just left to take our guests to their ship. The boys are not very well, and I stayed behind. What's wrong?" she asked sharply when he frowned.

He pointed beyond their property to the east and the rolling hills that gradually became steeper and covered with heavy forest to the horizon. Beth shielded her eyes from the morning sun and saw what she first thought was a low cloud. And then she knew.

"A bush fire!"

"Word came it must have started up during the night," he said briefly. "So far it is no real threat, but we are concerned it may spread quickly if the wind increases, and that is very likely." He looked toward the cow yards. "Is Henry still milking?"

"No, he has driven Mrs. MacGregor and Lucy into Adelaide. We needed several things, including supplies for our medicine cupboard," she explained briefly. "They left early so they could be home to do the milking tonight and prepare our evening meal."

Bob tipped his wide-brimmed hat back on his head and wiped the heavy film of perspiration from his forehead. "My whole family has already left."

Beth suddenly held her breath. He thought it was that serious?

"Bessie is taking the younger ones to safety closer to town, and the others have gone to fight the fire," he was saying briefly. "Perhaps when Henry returns, you would not mind if he checked on our place?"

He hesitated, and then added solemnly, "And tell Henry and your husband you would be best to keep the horses close by, even harnessed. Just in case, Mrs. Garrett."

He was gone before his final words had registered. Beth gave a frightened gasp and looked toward the hills. Surely the fire was too far away to be a real threat to them? Even as she looked, it seemed the cloud of smoke beyond the ridge of mountains was spreading wider, getting thicker.

She turned and ran inside.

When she had briefly told Miss Fisher what Bob had said, the lady turned pale. "I've heard dreadful stories of bush fires," she gasped and wrung her hands. "My brother even had to help fight one last year on the property he was working on."

"Good," Beth said briskly. "That means, I am sure, that he told you something of what they had to do."

Miss Fisher hesitated and then drew herself up and nodded. "I remember him saying that one of the problems was that the wind carried burning leaves and branches, often starting up fires wherever they landed miles away from the fire front."

Her voice faltered, and she bit her lip before continuing in a steadier voice. "We need water, plenty of water, blankets, bags, anything we can keep damp, anything we can use to beat out fire. Perhaps. . ." She gulped. "Perhaps we may even be able to wet the roof, although if the sun stays hot it will dry it out quickly."

She hesitated again, and then said in a voice that trembled just the slightest, "And do you think perhaps we should pack a few things just. . .just in case?"

Sudden fear swept through Beth. She sent up an urgent prayer. For a moment she stared at Miss Fisher, and then at last shook her head and said slowly. "No, not yet. The fire is still on the other side of the ridge. We'll get the water first. It is very still outside, so I don't think there is any danger at the moment from wind-driven embers, but we had better do what we can. Besides, everyone will be out fighting it so it may not even reach us."

She stopped. No matter what she thought, Bob Young was a levelheaded man. The risk. . .the risk of the fire reaching this far must be bad for all the Youngs to have left.

James started crying in the nursery, and they heard Harold's little patter as he talked to his brother.

The two women stared at each other silently. Beth saw her own fear reflected in Miss Fisher's eyes. They had no horses to help them flee. And they had two small boys to carry.

"We had best do all we can," Beth whispered at last, "just in case. And we will trust in God to look after us all."

She stepped forward, and the two women hugged each other. Catherine Fisher had always insisted on the formalities between mistress and servant, but all barriers were down now. They were merely two frightened women alone in a suddenly hostile environment.

Swiftly they organized themselves, taking turns watching the boys and drawing water from the new well to fill every container they could find. They collected as many items as they could think of that would beat out flames, and as they worked, both women kept glancing toward the east.

It was midday when they saw flames suddenly appear along the distant ridge, and to their horror, almost simultaneously the light easterly breeze increased considerably in strength. They could smell the smoke, and they watched as a few pieces of black leaves and ash flew into the yard.

"Do you think we should leave along the road and try to reach the river?" Beth panted after they had carried the last heavy bucket of water to the shade of the house.

"My brother said that the fires can swing around, can start up ahead of one from the flying embers and. . .and the heat drains all the air so you can hardly breathe." Catherine Fisher gave a frightened sob. "There is so much bush each side, the track is so narrow, and we would be far too slow. Besides, are you sure you know where the river is? What if we got lost?"

Beth stared at the bush, and knew Catherine was right. Her memory of being lost in the bush, stumbling through it while trying to find Harold had never left her. She looked around and was suddenly very, very glad William had insisted all the tall trees surrounding the house had been cleared in a wide circle. The intense heat of the past days had dried out the low bush, and the grass crackled under their feet.

"There is only one more thing we can do besides watching out for burning embers," she said sharply and raced to where the tools were kept.

They desperately raked as much of the twigs and dry grass as they could in a wide circle away from the house, and then set to with forks and spade diging up the ground to form some kind of firebreak. The ground was rock hard. Their hands soon blistered, and Beth had to agree at last that they were only wasting their energy.

All they could do was pour as much water on the roof of the house as they could and take turns keeping watch. And they prayed as they had all day.

When the first red-hot embers started falling, Beth went to gather what she could in the house and put it in the safest place. Where that might be she was not sure, she acknowledged grimly, but there were some things she would keep on her body.

She slumped wearily for a moment in the chair at William's desk before opening the drawer where she knew he kept their important personal papers. As she hurriedly slipped them into a large leather satchel, she suddenly spied some sheets of paper with William's scrawl on them. They were partly tucked under the large blotter on top of the desk.

No doubt important notes for his next sermon. She picked them up swiftly. She was wrong. Her own name caught her eye: *I Love You, Beth.*

A poem followed. It was the title of a love poem. Poetry. William had written a poem. A poem about her. Beth.

She stared at it, started to read. . .

> *I love you as birds love to fly*
>   *As desert flowers long for rain.*
> *I love you and my soul doth cry*
>   *For you to love me again.*
>
> *I loved you, but then I failed you*
>   *When my mind was reeling from fears.*
> *I loved you for remaining true*
>   *And turning my life with your tears.*
>
> *I love you for being my wife*
>   *You are, I know, God's gift to me.*
> *I love you, faithful in the strife*
>   *Caused by my own stupidities.*
>
> *I love you, with love more than mine*
>   *With a passion enriched by trust.*
> *I love you, Beth, with joy divine*
>   *Because our God did first love us.*
>
> *I love you, my sweet gentle Beth*
>   *With heartfelt longing, great pain.*
> *I love you, O beautiful Beth*
>   *And pray you'll embrace me again.*

It was the last few words, scrawled fiercely, the pencil almost piercing the paper, that brought the tears: *O God, how I love her! Forgive me. Cover me! Help her to forgive me. O God, how I love her!*

She sat, stunned. Then, her hand trembling, she turned over

the second sheet of paper. The title at the top declared it to be "My Three Loves."

Swiftly she read: *I love the Lord because He first loved me. His love is giving, my love is responding. His love is dying, my love is in living. His love is unchanging, my love is trembling. I love the Lord because He first loved me.*

In brackets he had scribbled 1 John 4:19. Beth had heard him quote that verse many times, but she stared at the words in wonder and then at last smiled mistily. She already knew this was how William loved his Lord. And his next love she also knew.

I love the Church because Christ gave Her Life. Betrothed Bride of Christ. Salvation's centerpiece. Through Her is Christ proclaimed. In Her, He is glorified. With Her He shall reign through all eternity—because Christ gave Her Life.

And then Beth caught her breath as she read the next line. . . and the next: *I love my wife because God gave her to me. A Grace gift to me to love, to cherish in all circumstances. She is wife and lover, my friend and coworker, mother to our children because God gave her to me.*

This was how the Reverend William Garrett loved his wife. As a precious gift from God. And she had dared to doubt his love!

Beth turned quickly back to that first precious page and was still staring at William's scrawl, trying to take in his beautiful words, when Catherine Fisher started screaming.

fourteen

William was eager to get back to Beth. Although she had been obviously distracted by the departure of Adam and Kate, as well as by the boys' slight fever, she had been unbelievably loving toward him all morning. And then there was her condition. . .

There had been all kinds of delays when they had arrived at Port Adelaide. It had taken much longer than they had expected to unload their baggage and ensure it was safely taken out to the ship. Other passengers had also decided to arrive early, and there had been long queues waiting in the hot sun for the longboats making several trips out to the ship at anchor offshore.

Eventually it had been Adam and Kate's turn. William had felt sad watching Adam and Kate disappear across the now-choppy waves of the gulf. The wind from the east had strengthened several hours before, and he knew it augured well for the commencement of their journey.

He had promised that one day his family would pay a return visit, even perhaps consider ministering at a church somewhere closer to them in New South Wales. But all of that required finding out what God wanted them to do, and at that Kate and Adam had smiled in perfect understanding, even if Kate had said fervently, "I'll certainly be having a few words to say to Him about it, though."

William wasted no time hitching up the horses and starting off. It was only after he had left the sandhills and the smell of the sea that he smelt the smoke. Uneasy, he stopped at the next rise and scanned the horizon. Only then did he see the distant gray wall of smoke. Relieved that it seemed well to the north of their area, he shook the reins and clucked to the horses to move off again, but with every mile the smoke became thicker and covered more of the sky. It seemed to be ominously close to their area.

With sudden fear, William remembered that Beth had insisted she and the nurse would manage perfectly well for a few hours while Henry took the other two women into town. He shook the reins and used the whip to start the horses running as they had never run pulling the carriage before. The further he traveled along the main road, the more people he met, their wagons piled up with all they could carry.

Not too far from the turnoff to their area, William suddenly recognized the cart pulled over to the side of the road and the girl standing on the seat peering back up the main road.

He pulled up swiftly, and Bessie Young turned her frightened, tear-streaked face toward him. "Oh, Mr. Williams, Mr. Williams, have you seen Ma and Pa?" she screamed.

He managed to calm her enough for her to sob out that they had been there for hours, expecting anytime to see her parents. "They all went to stop the fire spreading over the ridge, sir," she cried. "Pa told me to take the youngins and wait for them here on this wide road nearer to town. Just in case the fire got as far as our place. And now no one has been able to tell me any more than that it was heading directly toward us."

"You have been a very good girl, and you should perhaps go on closer to Adelaide now. Go to the church. I am sure there will be people there who will help you," William managed to say as calmly as he could, adding urgently, "Have you seen anybody from my place?"

"No, no, but Pa was going over there to get you to help them as we left this morning."

"This morning! When. . .Bessie, what time did your father send you off?"

When he heard the answer, William's heart pounded. His whole being was one prayer as he raced along the narrow track. Bob Young must only just have missed him! Each mile the panting, heaving horses drew closer, the smoke settled around him. The wind had dropped. Perhaps it would swing back. Perhaps the fire had missed them.

But as he topped the last rise, he groaned out loud. He was too late. The stables were blazing. From his viewpoint it looked like flames were shooting up from the house roof.

From that last hill to the house, the bush on each side of the track was still smouldering from the fire that had raced to devour and then sped on to search and claim more fuel in its relentless fury.

The horses' nostrils were flaring, their eyes showing their fear. William had difficulty controlling them as he forced them along through the smoke and heat, the smell of fire, until they at last stood trembling and snorting in the burned-out clearing surrounding the house. The stables had been consumed, the cow shed was still burning, and most of the fences were smouldering piles of ashes. Badly burned domestic and bush animals would have to be found, some to care for, others to put out of their misery.

But William hardly noticed or thought of them now. "Beth! Beth!" he croaked.

He was coughing, his eyes streaming from the smoke as he automatically tied up the frightened horses. Frantically he raced toward the house. Flames were shooting out from the windows of the kitchen. The roof caved in with a roar.

A section of the house nearest to the kitchen had just caught fire. Blackened figures formed a chain from the well to pass buckets of water to throw at the fire in a desperate fight against the enemy.

A small figure was up on the roof of the main house, frantically trying to put out a small fire that had just started. Someone else joined him, risking life and limb in a desperate attempt to save the whole house from going up.

One of the blackened figures near the kitchen gave a shout. William saw it was Robert Young and quickly joined him. "Beth, the boys," he gasped. "Are they safe?"

Robert shook his head. The soot-covered woman beside him panted desperately, "We don't know, but don't you dare say she is not safe somewhere, Bob Young! All our dear ones just have to be safe!"

And William realized it was Isabel Young, her legs clothed in an old pair of trousers, her hair tightly wrapped in an old scarf.

"I passed Bessie on the main road. They were very frightened but all safe. I sent them on into Adelaide," William said swiftly, relief sweeping through him. "Henry must have returned in time to get Beth."

Robert shook his head again. He grabbed the next bucket as he nodded toward the roof and panted breathlessly, "That's Henry. . .up on the roof. Only arrived a few minutes ago himself. Said. . .turned back. . .fire across the road. . .took your housekeeper and Lucy to safety. . .when he saw. . ."

But William had already gone. He raced around the house until he was as close as he could get to the frantically working little man above him and yelled, "Henry!"

A sudden gust of wind blew. It lifted some burning thatch from the kitchen, and sparks landed beside the small figure. Like a flash he jumped on them, desperately trying to extinguish the small flame before it could spread.

William saw the ladder Henry had dragged up to climb to the roof and was beside him as the last smouldering piece was sent hurtling down to the ground.

"A close one, boss." Henry smiled at him grimly but was flicking his hand, and William knew he must have burned himself. "The whole roof would have been long gone if it had not been so damp on this side."

A fit of coughing from the smoke choked William again, and before he had recovered enough to speak, Henry was saying urgently, "I'm so sorry I didn't get back in time. They had all gone. The fire. . .they must have tried to run away through the bush. I'm. . .I'm sorry. . ."

William stared at him, trying to take in what he was saying. Then a large tear trembled on the small man's rugged face, perhaps the first tear in a lifetime of harshness.

And William knew what he was saying. Miss Fisher, Beth, Harold, James. . .they could never have survived the intense heat, the smoke, the flames of the fire as it raced from treetop to treetop, consuming all in its path.

"No. . .no," William whispered. "I won't. . .I can't believe. . . Oh no!"

A faint, exhausted cheer went up from the people in the yard. The flames were dying down. The plowed ground of the vegetable paddock, even the pitifully small firebreak near the house, had slowed the fire until they had arrived. The barrels, the buckets, the kettles, even the kitchen saucepans filled with water had given the firefighters a head start, and now they had won the battle to save the house.

Even as they cheered, the strong wind was easing, changing direction, now more friend then foe. Later they would find that in the vagaries of a bush fire, it had somehow completely missed the Youngs' small property so close by.

Henry gave a deep, shuddering sigh. "We've won," he said with no sound of victory in his voice.

William was crouched with his head bowed, his strong shoulders shaking. "Oh, no, she. . .they. . .mean more than life to me. No. . .no," he said over and over in shock.

A firm hand landed on his shoulder. He ignored it, and then it shook him hard. Henry's shaking, wondering voice whispered, "Look. . .look, boss. Through the smoke."

William raised his head and stared blindly at Henry. Then he looked numbly where the man's hand was pointing.

Two figures were moving like shadows through the smoke. They slowly stumbled into sight, dodging around burning tree stumps, disappearing into pockets of smoke, but ever getting closer until Henry and William's straining eyes could see them more clearly.

William had stiffened and stared, his eyes hardly daring to believe. And then he moved. Across the roof. Down the ladder. And running. . .and running. . .

Henry gave a great shout. The exhausted people on the ground looked up at him. At his pointing hand. They turned. A gasp went up as a tall, black man grasping the wrist of a short, slight figure stumbled into view.

Another tall, desperately racing man had nearly reached them. The aboriginal gave a grunt and let go of the woman. She gave a faint cry before she flung herself forward and was enclosed in strong, loving arms.

Only a few noticed the black man gaze for a moment toward the group of people near the house. But neither noticed him slip silently away, back through the burned-out bush and into the gray wall of smoke. All eyes were on the couple standing as one.

"Oh, William, William, you're safe!"

Words were beyond him. She was safe! All he could do was hold her to his shaking, gasping body, and then push her back to look into her eyes with a desperate question in his own.

"We are all safe," Beth told him swiftly, her words tumbling over, trying to reassure him. "Harold, James, Catherine. The aboriginal woman and her man came and made us all go with them to the river, to a wide water hole. They came racing up to the house and frightened Catherine badly at first.

"We did not want to go. But the woman screamed over and over that word I told you about, 'Kawai.' The man grabbed up Harold, even prodded us with his spear until we were running and running. We. . .we did not realize the fire was so close, coming so fast," she panted. "We made it into the water just in time. Oh, it was dreadful! We never realized. . .it came so fast. I could never believe the fury of it, the heat. It was so hard to breathe. We crouched up to our necks in the water in the middle of a huge water hole while the fire burned all around us."

She gave a loud sob and started to shake. "We. . .the boys. . . would not have survived that heat here. Catherine. . .she. . .has stayed with the boys, the woman, and their son because the smoke is still so dense, while I. . .I. . .I had to make sure you were safe!"

He was holding her again so tightly she could not speak, could hardly breathe. Nothing mattered but that she was safe. Together they would rebuild what was lost in the fire. Together they would love and serve their God in this Great Southland.

And at last he found his voice. "I thought I had lost you," he groaned, and she felt his tears against her face. "Oh, Beth, I love you more than life."

A shuddering sigh swept through Beth. "I know, my darling William, I know," she whispered.

Her hands were soothing him, wiping away the moisture that still flowed down his strong, smoke-stained face, and at last he drew one more deep breath and slowly raised his head to devour her filthy, soot- and smoke-blackened face with his eyes. Some of her hair was singed, making him realize how close the danger had been.

"And I love you more than life itself, my husband," she whispered at long last, knowing now the words to use to convince him.

The brilliance of the light that flashed into William's eyes and spread across his face awed Beth. She knew that their love would last through the years. Because what William had written had been so true.

Their love for each other had been given by the very source of love. They loved because God in Christ had first loved them. Their love for each other was a precious gift of sheer grace from the God who is love. And this kind of love would never fade, just grow richer and deeper.

Later there would be hours of talking, as they should have talked over the years. He would tell her about being so nervous when he asked to speak to Lord Farnley privately, intending to ask for her hand in marriage. Instead, he found himself being rushed into that appalling arranged wedding and then feeling dreadfully guilty about the whole affair because he believed she had been pressured into it. He would confess the jealousy, the hatred he had fought not to have toward John, until he had been able to allow God to love John through him, even before he knew the truth.

She would tell him that she now knew how selfish and immature she had been when they married, how childishly foolish. They would laugh joyfully together that as he had been marrying two strangers, she had finally realized the true nature of her love. He would admit that he had come so close that same day to damaging their reputation by publicly hauling her into his arms and kissing her senseless beneath the tall gum tree!

She would share with him that she had realized it was her nature and upbringing that made her feel shy about talking publicly about deep spiritual issues, yet her own trust and love for God had grown over the years. And he would kiss her again with a loving groan when she informed him emphatically that this was due mainly to the Christian life he lived before her each day.

Shyly she would ask the question that had puzzled her for months. How had he not known on their wedding night there had been no other lover? She would delight in the tide of color that swept into his face as he briefly muttered that it had been because he himself had been totally innocent and could not judge the matter. And she knew that it had been because of his incredible gentleness and care of her that night as well.

He would tell her that despite the temptations he had faced when men upheld standards for women they did not keep for themselves, it had been easy for him to resist because of his love for her and his determination to obey God's Word.

But that was all still to come. None of it mattered at this glorious moment. Now they were smiling radiantly at each other, and Beth put it all into words.

"Because God loved us first, we love," she whispered tenderly. "He gave you to me, me to you, 'Grace gifts' to love and cherish in all circumstances, for all eternity."

And in the end, the telling and the knowing was as simple as that.

epilogue

In 1840, transportation of convicts to New South Wales ceased. But just as it ended in the east of Australia, it began in the west. It was not until January 10, 1868, that the last convict ship to Australia landed at Fremantle, eighty years to the month since the First Fleet dropped anchor in Sydney Cove to colonize the Great Southland.

South Australia is the only state that never had convicts transported to its shores to help establish the settlement. Adelaide has often been called "The City of Churches."

The early pioneers faced many hardships. Although all other characters in this story are fictitious, where the Telfer and Pedler names have been used, the incidents are based on actual events.

The Pedlers and Telfers are perhaps typical of so many who had the courage to voluntarily leave their homes to try and establish better lives for their children. Jean Telfer died just twenty-six days after arriving in Adelaide. Her husband, Francis, married their shipboard friend Dinah Flavel in November 1839. In March 1844, at the age of twenty-three, Dinah also died. Three months after Dinah's death, Jean and Francis's twelve-year-old son, James, went missing, and his body was never found. Francis married again. John, the first child of this marriage to Margaret, was my mother's grandfather.

The Pedler family also had their share of tragedies. William the Third's brother Joseph died in 1845 of consumption, which may have developed in the damp conditions of a mine in Cornwall years before. I have discovered that he had a granddaughter who was called Mary Ellen Pedler, my own name!

William and his brother Thomas were shoemakers for some

years and then farmers. The child born to Elizabeth Pedler in May 1839 was Nicholas, my father's grandfather.

Down through the decades, branches of both families moved to Eyre's Peninsula to pioneer farming around the Tumby Bay and Ungarra area. And then one day, two people who loved and served Jesus Christ, Les Pedler and Gladys Telfer, were married. They also inherited the pioneer spirit and in 1939 were among the first wheat growers on the Darling Downs in Queensland.

I am very proud to be their daughter, Mary.

A Letter To Our Readers

Dear Reader:

In order that we might better contribute to your reading enjoyment, we would appreciate your taking a few minutes to respond to the following questions. We welcome your comments and read each form and letter we receive. When completed, please return to the following:

Rebecca Germany, Fiction Editor
Heartsong Presents
PO Box 719
Uhrichsville, Ohio 44683

1. Did you enjoy reading *Love in the Great Southland?*
   ❑ Very much. I would like to see more books
      by this author!
   ❑ Moderately
      I would have enjoyed it more if _____

      _____

      _____

2. Are you a member of **Heartsong Presents**? Yes ❑ No ❑
   If no, where did you purchase this book? _____

   _____

3. How would you rate, on a scale from 1 (poor) to 5 (superior), the cover design? _____

4. On a scale from 1 (poor) to 10 (superior), please rate the following elements.

   _____ Heroine   _____ Plot

   _____ Hero   _____ Inspirational theme

   _____ Setting   _____ Secondary characters

5. These characters were special because_____

_____

_____

6. How has this book inspired your life?_____

_____

_____

7. What settings would you like to see covered in future
   Heartsong Presents books?_____

_____

_____

8. What are some inspirational themes you would like to see
   treated in future books?_____

_____

_____

9. Would you be interested in reading other **Heartsong
   Presents** titles?   Yes ❏   No ❏

10. Please check your age range:
    ❏ Under 18   ❏ 18-24   ❏ 25-34
    ❏ 35-45   ❏ 46-55   ❏ Over 55

11. How many hours per week do you read?_____

Name _____

Occupation _____

Address _____

City _____ State _____ Zip _____

Discover the joy of love...

A nostalgic look at springtimes past, and the joy of love discovered. *Spring's Memory* is the latest collection of historical inspirational novellas from Barbour Publishing. Includes the stories *A Valentine for Prudence* by Darlene Mindrup, *Set Sail My Heart* by Colleen Coble, *The Wonder of Spring* by Carol Cox, and *The Blessings Basket* by Judith McCoy Miller.

400 pages, Paperbound, 5 ³⁄₁₆" x 8"

❤ ❤ ❤ ❤ ❤ ❤ ❤ ❤ ❤ ❤ ❤ ❤ ❤ ❤ ❤ ❤

❤ ❤ ❤ ❤ ❤ ❤ ❤ ❤ ❤ ❤ ❤ ❤ ❤ ❤ ❤ ❤

·····Hearts♥ng·······

HEARTSONG PRESENTS TITLES AVAILABLE NOW:

·········· Presents ··········

__HP272 ALBERT'S DESTINY, *Birdie L. Etchision*

__HP275 ALONG UNFAMILIAR PATHS, *Amy Rognlie*

__HP276 THE MOUNTAIN'S SON, *Gloria Brandt*

__HP279 AN UNEXPECTED LOVE, *Andrea Boeshaar*

__HP280 A LIGHT WITHIN, *Darlene Mindrup*

__HP283 IN LIZZY'S IMAGE, *Carolyn R. Scheidies*

__HP284 TEXAS HONOR, *Debra White Smith*

__HP287 THE HOUSE ON WINDRIDGE, *Tracie Peterson*

__HP288 SWEET SURRENDER, *JoAnn A. Grote*

__HP291 REHOBOTH, *DiAnn Mills*

__HP292 A CHILD OF PROMISE, *Jill Stengl*

__HP295 TEND THE LIGHT, *Susannah Hayden*

__HP296 ONCE MORE CHANCE, *Kimberley Comeaux*

__HP299 EM'S ONLY CHANCE, *Rosey Dow*

__HP300 CHANGES OF THE HEART, *Judith McCoy Miller*

__HP303 MAID OF HONOR, *Carolyn R. Scheidies*

__HP304 SONG OF THE CIMARRON, *Kelly R. Stevens*

__HP307 SILENT STRANGER, *Peggy Darty*

__HP308 A DIFFERENT KIND OF HEAVEN, *Tammy Shuttlesworth*

__HP311 IF THE PROSPECT PLEASES, *Sally Laity*

__HP312 OUT OF THE DARKNESS, *Dianna Crawford and Rachel Druten*

__HP315 MY ENEMY, MY LOVE, *Darlene Mindrup*

__HP316 FAITH IN THE GREAT SOUTHLAND, *Mary Hawkins*

__HP319 MARGARET'S QUEST, *Muncy Chapman*

__HP320 HOPE IN THE GREAT SOUTHLAND, *Mary Hawkins*

__HP323 NO MORE SEA, *Gloria Brandt*

__HP324 LOVE IN THE GREAT SOUTHLAND, *Mary Hawkins*

Great Inspirational Romance at a Great Price!

Heartsong Presents books are inspirational romances in contemporary and historical settings, designed to give you an enjoyable, spirit-lifting reading experience. You can choose wonderfully written titles from some of today's best authors like Peggy Darty, Sally Laity, Tracie Peterson, Colleen L. Reece, Lauraine Snelling, and many others.

When ordering quantities less than twelve, above titles are $2.95 each.
Not all titles may be available at time of order.

SEND TO: Heartsong Presents Reader's Service
P.O. Box 719, Uhrichsville, Ohio 44683

Please send me the items checked above. I am enclosing $_____.
(please add $1.00 to cover postage per order. OH add 6.25% tax. NJ add 6%). Send check or money order, no cash or C.O.D.s, please.
To place a credit card order, call 1-800-847-8270.

NAME _____

ADDRESS _____

CITY/STATE _____ ZIP _____

HPS 4-99

Heartsong Presents
Love Stories Are Rated G!

That's for godly, gratifying, and of course, great! If you love a thrilling love story, but don't appreciate the sordidness of some popular paperback romances, **Heartsong Presents** is for you. In fact, **Heartsong Presents** is the *only inspirational romance book club*, the only one featuring love stories where Christian faith is the primary ingredient in a marriage relationship.

Sign up today to receive your first set of four, never before published Christian romances. Send no money now; you will receive a bill with the first shipment. You may cancel at any time without obligation, and if you aren't completely satisfied with any selection, you may return the books for an immediate refund!

Imagine. . .four new romances every four weeks—two historical, two contemporary—with men and women like you who long to meet the one God has chosen as the love of their lives. . .all for the low price of $9.97 postpaid.

To join, simply complete the coupon below and mail to the address provided. **Heartsong Presents** romances are rated G for another reason: They'll arrive *Godspeed!*